# Idea Sparking
## Brainstorming Conflict to Deepen Your Novel

## By Michelle Lim

# My Book Therapy
### Grand Marais, MN

ISBN-10: 0984696963

ISBN-13: 978-0-9846969-6-3

Visit our Website at www.mybooktherapy.com for information on more resources for writers.

To receive instruction on writing or further help with writing projects via My Book Therapy's fiction editing services, contact info@ mybooktherapy.com.

Designed by: David C. Warren

Edited by: Susan May Warren

# DEDICATION

To my grandmother, Barbara Helm whose love of story

gave me the opportunity to read countless

novels from her book clubs.

~~~

To my mom, who taught me how to plot and believed in me

even before I believed in myself. And my Dad

who gave his time to help me write.

~~~

To my husband who has supported my dream

and cheered me on every step of the way!

~~~

To my children who asked me every day if I was pugalished

and shared mom with her imaginary characters.

# Special Thanks:

**Susan May Warren**- You give selflessly to others without caring who gets the credit. You gave me the courage to believe I could be a writer and the tools to apply to my work. Thank you a million times over for being your amazing, inspiring self.

**The My Book Therapy Editing Team**- Susan May Warren and David Warren, thank you so much for all of your hard work and dedication on this project. Your encouragement and enthusiasm inspired me to be a better writer.

**Annette Irby**- Thank you for your additional edits to help me add polish to my book.

**Lisa Jordan**- Thank you for being my Cliff Whisperer and craft partner throughout my writing journey. I would not be published if it weren't for you.

**My Friends and Crit Partners**- Rachel Hauck, Amanda Stephens, Beth K. Vogt, Cynthia Ruchti, Amy Lindberg, Pat Trainum, Edie Melson, Alena Tauriainen , Reba Hoffman, Melissa Tagg, and Jeannie Shattuck. It is through the support of others that we are strong. You have made me stronger.

**Minnesota N.I.C.E.-** Thanks for giving me the opportunity to grow as a writer and enjoy the fellowship of friends along the way.

# Contents

# Introduction

As a writer, sometimes you feel as if you've entered a world as foreign as Mars and as complicated as a foreign language. I know exactly how you feel. I've been there so many times that I'm earning frequent flyer miles on Baffled Writer Airlines. Every ounce of energy poured into your manuscript hasn't landed you a contract, or it hasn't put you on the bestseller list like you'd hoped. What you need is that last burst of inspiration that will push your story from good to great, your characters from empathetic to loveable.

Agents and editors receive thousands of manuscripts a year. Standing out in that crowd is as difficult as making the top ten on American Idol. You may be a good writer, you many know the craft, but unless you have something unique to offer the reader you will likely stay in the slush pile. Not only will you be in the slush pile, but scores of others will join the pile on top of your manuscript and your chances of a contract go down immensely.

How do you find that spark, that burst of inspiration creating brilliance where average used to be? Fresh and unique ideas with layers of surprises that delight editors and readers alike will lift you out of the slush pile and into the possibility zone. Now, your writing and wordsmithing can shine to bring you the recognition you crave.

Have you ever tried rubbing two sticks together to start a fire? You can rub those sticks together over and over, but without that first spark there is no fire. If you want your book to catch fire and spread like wildfire, you need to generate sparks. It may take more than one, maybe several, but sparks are essential to building a fire.

Ideas are the sparks in a novel. A rich bank of ideas allows the writer to explore beyond the predictable and reach for the unexpected. When we author has several ideas to choose from, our stories become much more complex. We often reach for the plot that is less simple if we have choices. The trick is creating those idea choices.

Whether you have blank page paralysis or are a plotting guru, your story and characters can be layered with complexity if you create idea sparks. One of the most important processes for idea sparking is brainstorming. Not just before you write your novel, not just if you are a plotter, not just if you have writer's block, brainstorming is critical to all writers.

I'm what I call a purposeful pantser. I make sure I have the basics to the character journey and the key plot elements. I know where the story will end, but then I sit down to write. I love the moment when I open up the closet and a character is inside hiding, only I didn't know that would happen a few minutes before.

So you might think that a pantser doesn't need to brainstorm because they already are great at coming up with plot. WRONG. Pantsers need idea sparks just as much as the plotter because there are many opportunities in a novel to be predictable. Even if your next action is unpredictable, that doesn't mean it is the most powerful way to tell your story.

Idea sparking is essential for all writers who want their stories to catch on like wildfire. Brainstorming is the key that unlocks your mind to out-of-the box ideas and fills your page with depth.

Not everyone is a natural born brainstormer, but with the strategies you will learn in this book you will be brainstorming to spark ideas with ease. These strategies can be used by published and unpublished authors alike at different points in your novel. You can brainstorm ideas. If you don't know how yet, you will before this book is finished.

The focus of this book is to brainstorm conflict ideas that will create unpredictable plot, trim up that sagging middle and avoid overused story line. Each strategy will target a different kind of roadblock that you can brainstorm ideas about to create more conflict in your novel.

Once you've learned these strategies, you can keep this book handy for moments when you need sparks and pick a strategy to implement. It will start you on a new adventure to the way you think about writing and serve as a resource to refer to at difficult times.

Our Amazing Creator has blessed you with a mind so rich and full of ideas that you haven't even begun to explore. Now is your chance. Are you ready to transform your story by brainstorming conflict idea sparks? Great! Let's get started.

# PART ONE
## Basic Components of Idea Sparking

# Packing Flint

Any survival expert could tell you that being able to start a fire if you are stranded in the wild is extremely important. It provides a source of heat, wards off predators, allows you to cook and dry out wet clothing. All of that from one source. Because fire is so valuable to the adventurer many hikers or campers pack flint. Flint is a type of rock that when struck with metal creates sparks.

One little spark is all it takes sometimes to start a fire. It is the same with our brainstorming ideas. One little spark can start a whole new line of plot conflict that fuels our story to bonfire proportions.

Brainstorming is the flint that sparks ideas. It will get the flames going when you're stranded in a predictable plot or staring at a blank page. It fuels the development of layers and depth in your story.

So, how can you create ideas when you're not a strong brainstormer? Start by realizing you already have what it takes inside of you. Flint is a great fire starter, but if you don't strike it against anything else, it won't produce sparks. It will just sit there and stare back at you. It takes the effort of striking the flint against something else to create the sparks.

Becoming a strong brainstormer takes effort, just like flint needs to strike against something else to ignite a flame. There are a couple of basic principles to opening your mind to whatever ideas you may think up. If you follow them, in time you will become a stronger brainstormer.

## Basic Brainstorming Principles

**Don't Censor Your Ideas.** This is one area that I believe is the most crippling to writers. We must allow ourselves to blurt without judgment, any thought that goes through our mind. At this stage there aren't good ideas and bad ideas, there are just ideas. Not all rocks are flint, but that doesn't mean we go out to the rock pile and criticize the rest of the rocks for being themselves. Allow your mind to explore all ideas without judging them.

**Blurt In A Continuous Stream.** Let the ideas roll without any thought in between. Remember, you aren't judging the worthiness of the ideas. Just say them or write them down freely.

**Don't Stop Too Early.** You may have come up with a great idea, but don't stop there. Keep blurting. You never know what other great ideas will come out. One of them might be better than the first one, or may be something you can use later on. Oftentimes the first thought that comes to our minds is predictable or cliché. Push past those initial ideas and you might find flint.

**Brainstorm in Small Chunks.** If you've ever heard the phrase, "Don't bite off more than you can chew," that would sum up this concept. Brainstorming should be about small things in the story. An object, a character, an event, etc. Don't try to figure out everything at once, or you will just come up with general ideas. What you really want is more specific ideas.

# Practical Application

We are going to apply these rules to a very simple exercise. You are going to brainstorm everything you think about the topic below for three minutes. It doesn't matter what you blurt, just whatever that idea makes you think about. Ready. Set. Go.

**Apples**

| | | |
|---|---|---|
| *Johnny Appleseed* | *Bite* | *Candy* |
| *Orchard Tree* | *Kids* | *Healthy* |
| *Red* | *Bobbing* | *Crunchy* |
| *Yellow* | *Apple* | *Lunch* |
| *Sweet* | *Halloween* | *Fruit* |

As you can see, some of the ideas are a bit on the edges. For example, when I thought of bobbing for apples, the word Halloween popped into my head. I could have said, "Wait a minute. That is not about apples," and not put that on my list. If I eliminated this from my list, I would have censored my thoughts...

Let's see what impact that could have on my character. If Sally is a ten-year-old girl who doesn't like apples and in the story many mishaps occur because of it, I might brainstorm about apples (notice it is a very small part of the story). If I crossed Halloween off of my list, I would miss the opportunity to include a bobbing for apples Halloween dilemma. I censored my way right out of a perfectly solid conflict to introduce to my character.

Let's Try It Again. No censoring.

**Football Game**

| | | |
|---|---|---|
| Quarterback | Gatorade | Quiet |
| Linemen | field | loud |
| Wide Receiver | White Chalk | blue wig |
| Touchdown | whistle | stripes |
| Penalty | Ball | Zebra |
| Foul | pigskin | chest painting |
| Roughing the Passer | field goal | tailgating |
| Coach | soccer | mascot |

We could keep going, but do you see how many varied ideas came to mind? A football game isn't quiet, but for some reason that word came to my mind. And what's with the zebra? Well, that would be the striped shirt of the umpire that reminded me of a zebra. Sure, sometimes the ideas I blurt don't make sense or won't work, but that doesn't exclude them from the list.

Think for a moment if my character was a quarterback and during the game a zebra ran out on the field. Of course you would have to make this believable, but what great fringe plot. What if, in a crime investigation, white chalk was found on the suspect's clothing? Gatorade could be something I might smell in a scene. What if I were chased by the blue-wigged fan with a painted chest?

As you can see, following those basic brainstorming rules can bring out unique ideas that never crossed your mind before. Do you see anything unexpected on your list? If not, keep doing this activity with various objects or people. The more you practice, the better you will get at brainstorming. Refining your flint talents with practice will revitalize your writing. Once you have packed your brainstorming flint, you are ready to spark ideas and help your story catch on like wildfire.

As we get started on our idea sparking journey remember to pack flint. Be ready to strike it against something else. Be ready to fan the flame.

# Finding Tinder

You've packed your flint and are ready for your adventure in Idea Sparking, but a few more items are needed to prepare you for the journey. One of those essentials is tinder. Tinder is the collection of things you find in your setting to use as fuel. Without this, you can send sparks flying as much as you want, but you won't start a fire.

What is the tinder in our novels? It is the basic goals we have set up for our character, or what they are trying to achieve and the stakes, or why it matters. Introducing idea sparks without the framework of character goals and stakes creates a plot that lacks conflict.

Conflicts are the roadblocks to your character's goals in the story. Some conflict affects one scene, other conflict affects multiple scenes. In individual scenes these roadblocks are called obstacles. These obstacles, or conflicts stand in the way of your character reaching their scene goals.

There are three key components to each scene that will set up the framework for conflict: Goals, Obstacles, and Stakes. These three components create Tinder for the fire.

## The Three Tier Framework for Building Meaningful Conflict:

**Goals:** This is the POV Character's goal in the scene, or what the character wants. (Not the author goal.)

**Obstacles:** Things that get in the way of the POV Character achieving their scene goal.

**Stakes:** What is at stake for them in this scene? What will happen if they don't achieve their goal?

## Tier One: Goals

Goals are one of the most important parts of the start of each scene. It gives the scene direction and determines the focus for conflict. If you were going on a family vacation, would you just get in the car and drive aimlessly? Of course not. So, why would we write aimlessly? This is where your character goal comes into play. Oftentimes writers mix up their author goals with their character goals. So let me start by clarifying them.

**Author Goal:** What you as an author want to accomplish in a scene. For example, showing home world, or lie they believe, or to give a specific plot clue.

**Character Goal:** This is the Point of View Character's goal for the scene. What are they trying to do? Usually it comes at the beginning of a scene. You should know the direction in the first few paragraphs.

**Example:** If Callie didn't find that paper in the next ten minutes, she'd die today. She wouldn't give up until she knew exactly where she'd left the ransom drop point directions. Ransom for her own life. Now that was a first.

The POV Character in this scene is Callie. Her Goal: To find the ransom drop point directions.

As an Author your goal might be to hook the reader and give them a reason to read on, to make the reader wonder why they need to give a ransom for themselves.

When you read through the first few paragraphs of a scene, you should be able to tell what the POV character's goal is for the scene. If you can't find that, then you won't recognize conflict opportunities when you see them. Who cares if someone calls her and takes up her time? It doesn't matter unless she has a deadline and in this case life or death stakes. Without a character goal all of the conflict you introduce in a scene falls flat. Instead the reader is left to meander and enjoy the story on the stage, but they may not care about what happens to your character or see the significance of the conflicts you are introducing.

## Practical Application

**Identify the character goal in the following story clip.**

*The time for sorry vanished with his '65 Chevy, but that didn't mean she'd wait for him to come back. The next bus left at 2 o'clock and she aimed to be on it. No hundred mile stretch of highway could stand between them. She'd be outside of his apartment by 4 in the afternoon, or her grandma wasn't a gun toting red neck.*

**What is the Character Goal?**

_____

_____

_____

## Tier Two: Obstacles

Now that you have a POV Character goal for the scene, you have the framework to add the obstacles or roadblocks to the character reaching their goals. Think of your scene as a race. Your character is at the starting line. The finish line is reaching their goals. Everything between the start and finish that makes it difficult for the character to reach their goals are called obstacles.

Let's look again at the example of Callie:

*If Callie didn't find that paper in the next ten minutes, she'd die today. She wouldn't give up until she knew exactly where she'd left the ransom drop point directions. Ransom for her own life. Now that was a first.*

Callie's goal is to find the directions for the ransom drop point in the next ten minutes. So, we need to give her obstacles in the scene to achieving that goal.

**Possibilities:** A phone call from her mother who has terminal cancer. (Notice I had to make that call a bit important. Callie needed a reason to not want to hang up on her mom for it to be a bigger obstacle. Just a plain phone call would work, but adding that extra tension makes it better.)

**OR:** She spills coffee all over her desk papers where she believes the directions are sitting. (This takes extra time to dry things off, but also the directions could be ruined. Aim for a double slam on the obstacles.)

**OR:** A police officer comes to the door with questions about the disappearance of a neighbor. (Here is another example of a double slam obstacle. The person at the door is not just anyone, but a Police Officer investigating a crime. She can't blow him off easily without him feeling suspicious.)

Select a few obstacles for your character to face that keeps them from their goal. The more double slam obstacles you have, the better. Your character's goal could change in the middle of the scene if you want. Maybe they don't reach their goal, but you need the plot to feed off of obstacles.

## Practical Application

What are other obstacles Callie could face in this scene that keep her from her goals?

_____

_____

_____

_____

## *Tier Three: Stakes*

Stakes simply provide the answer to why the goal matters. The higher the stakes, the more your reader will care. Be sure the stakes are something that logically matter to your character and most often your reader.

Notice in the example of Callie, the stakes are her life. If she didn't find the directions in ten minutes she would die. Life stakes are big. You can't have life stakes in every scene, but it helps to have the stakes in the first scene huge enough to grab your reader. And the stakes in all of your scenes should make the reader care and feel worried the character won't reach their goals.

# Practical Application

What things could be at stake for your character that she and your readers might care about?

_____

_____

_____

_____

_____

_____

_____

_____

_____

_____

As we've discovered, the three-tier framework for creating mean-ingful conflict in your novel is an important structure to allow the tinder to ignite. The tinder or the character's goal is the fuel that makes meaningful conflict possible.

## Recognizing the Framework:

As we get ready to use idea sparking to brainstorm different conflict opportunities in our novels, it is important to recognize the framework that makes these conflicts meaningful. Before brainstorming conflicts, it is helpful to determine the goals the character is trying to achieve so you can ensure the conflict packs punch.

Read the following mini-excerpt and identify the three-tier framework for conflict:

*Dying didn't give her the right to condemn someone else, but being a mother did. Daphne looked across the sitting room at the oiliest, most corrupt man in all of Millner's Grove, her son-in-law. The scent of his cigars clogged her throat. It was time to change the will, before he got his grubby hands on her daughter's fortune.*

*"You aren't looking well today, Daphne. Can I get you anything?" Raymond's plastic grin didn't meet his eyes.*

*"You could leave." She smoothed her white collar shirt, wrinkled hands stopping on the broach at her throat. He couldn't have a cent of it. Her Thomas' fortune must remain safe. If she could just get rid of the snake, she'd call her attorney and get things settled before nightfall.*

*"I could, but what kind of son-in-law would I be, if I left you all alone in this big house? Why, something unfortunate might happen."*

*"Suit yourself. But if you don't mind, I have some business to conduct." Daphne snagged the phone off of the mahogany desk and dialed a number. The dead air filled her ears. The storm must have damaged the phone lines, unless...*

*Raymond hadn't left. He stood next to the red velvet drapes and peaked out between the creases at the heavy clouds ready to open* up and pour out their fury on the earth. His skeletal hands clung to the drapes for a brief moment before yanking them closed.

Daphne looked at the grandfather clock that stood near the door. Her daughter wouldn't be home for another hour and a half. Daphne opened the top right drawer of her desk and felt inside for her husband's pistol.

"Looking for this." Raymond held up the pistol in his hands. A sneer covered his face. His suit couldn't hide the smug angle of his shoulders. "It's really too bad you couldn't have been as easy to fool as your daughter. It's your own fault really."

"So what, now you're going to kill me?" Her voice trembled slightly. She caught a breath.

"No, darling. You are going to kill you."

The following story clip will help you recognize the goals, obstacles and stakes in a scene. The framework in this scene is illustrated below.

**Author Goal:** To show the evil of the son-in-law and hook the reader at the beginning of the book.

**POV Character Goals:** To get her son-in-law out of the will. To protect her family's fortune and her daughter. To contact the lawyer today.

**Obstacles:** Her son-in-law won't leave and the phone lines are dead. Her daughter won't be home for another hour and a half. Raymond has her gun.

**Stakes:** Losing the family fortune and her daughter's safety. She is also afraid for her own life (at the end only—technically not a huge part of the drive forward in this scene because we don't know until the end that this is at stake).

If we hadn't given the goals, obstacles, or stakes in this scene, the conflict would lack punch. Read how it might have read:

*Dying didn't give her the right to condemn someone else, but being a mother did. Daphne looked across the sitting room at the oiliest, most corrupt man in all of Millner's Grove, her son-in-law. The scent of his cigars clogged her throat.*

*"You aren't looking well today, Daphne. Can I get you anything?" Raymond's plastic grin didn't meet his eyes.*

*"You could leave." She smoothed her white collar shirt, wrinkled hands stopping on the broach at her throat.*

*"I could, but what kind of son-in-law would I be, if I left you all alone in this big house? Why, something unfortunate might happen."*

*"Suit yourself. But if you don't mind, I have some business to conduct." Daphne snagged the phone off of the mahogany desk and dialed a number. No answer. Raymond hadn't left. He stood next to the red velvet drapes and peaked out between the creases at the heavy clouds ready to open up and pour out their fury on the earth. His skeletal hands clung to the drapes for a brief moment before yanking them closed.*

*Daphne looked at the grandfather clock that stood near the door.*

*A sneer covered Raymond's face. His suit couldn't hide the smug angle of his shoulders. "It's really too bad you couldn't have been as easy to fool as your daughter. It's your own fault really."*

*"So what, now you're going to kill me?" Her voice trembled slightly. She caught a breath.*

*"No, darling. You are going to kill you."*

You can see that without the three-tier framework for creating meaningful conflict the scene is much flatter. At the end of the scene we do have a bit of conflict from the plot, but without the other components, this plot moment loses some of its impact.

## Practical Application:

Now that you have seen the importance of Stakes, Obstacles, and Goals, it's time to try building them into one of your scenes. Pick a scene from your novel and fill in the information below.

**What is your POV Character's Goal for this scene?**

_____

_____

_____

_____

**What are some obstacles that can get in the way of your character reaching their goal?**

_____

_____

_____

_____

**What is at stake for your character in this scene?**

_____

_____

_____

_____


**Can you intensify any of the stakes so they become double slams?**

_____

_____

_____

_____

Using the three-tier framework for creating meaningful conflict we have discover the tinder, or character goals necessary to start a fire. We have two components of a three part equation:

Brainstorming is the combination of:

**Flint + Tinder + ? = Fire**

**OR**

**Ideas + Character Goals + Stakes + ? = Fire**

Now that you have learned the first two components, let's find out how to make the fire start so we can begin to look at specific Conflict Brainstorming Strategies.

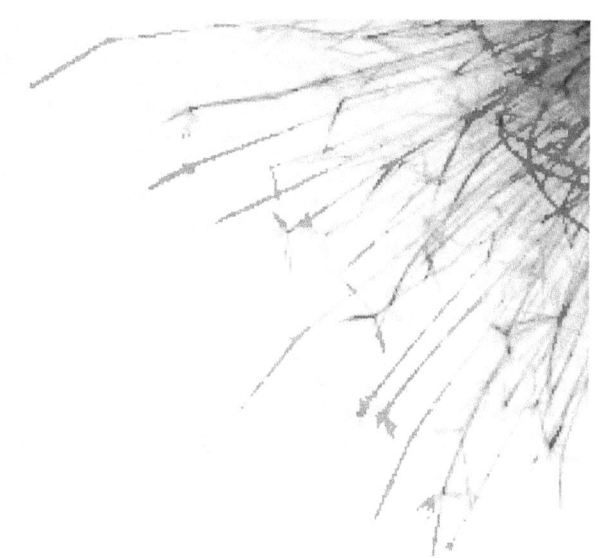

# Let the Sparks Fly

We have packed the flint or our brainstorming prowess, we searched for tinder or our character's goals and stakes, now we need something to strike against the flint to create sparks. In the woods, another rock or a piece of metal you brought along might work. In our manuscripts the sparks are conflict ideas that create the necessary friction to build a fire.

Conflicts, as we learned in the previous chapter, are the roadblocks our characters face while trying to reach their goals. Conflict can be carried in a single scene or over a large number of scenes like you might find in a story where the heroine is trying to escape a killer. In our novels, part of the conflict that feeds our plots stem from both inside and outside of a character.

A balance of internal or inside conflict and external or outside conflict gives a book a stronger punch when it is based on what the character wants to achieve. Imagine yourself on the first day at a new high school. You've put on the latest fashion that your mom said cost her whole paycheck. You stand at the end of your driveway waiting for a large yellow monster, I mean school bus to swallow you up. The thoughts are racing through your head. How will I ever fit in? What if nobody likes me? Do I have cornflakes stuck in my teeth?

At that moment you are dealing with all kinds of internal conflict because you want to fit in. This conflict arises from what you want to achieve and the related emotions inside of you. All of the turmoil you are feeling builds the internal conflict.

Just when you think things couldn't get worse, your brother slaps his sneaker into a puddle, splashing mud all over your new jeans. You look at your watch. There is no time to change into a clean outfit You'll just have to go to school grungy.

At this moment you are dealing with external conflict—your brother getting your jeans dirty and the timetable not allowing you to go inside of the house and change. These two conflicts come from the outside of you.

The brother showing up on the scene might be an example of fringe plotting (when something comes from the outside edges of the story to impact your story's plot). Fringe plotting is a way to create external conflict.

Then you have the time factor. The lack of time available to go back and change is also external, it is something that happens outside of you that you can't control, but it adds conflict to the story. Both of these are examples of external conflict.

The bus stops in front of you and you get on. *I just hope they don't call me mud puppy, or laugh at my clothes. What if I end up in the loser crowd? We should never have moved from Centerville. I've got to convince my parents to move back.*

Your character here is dealing with all kinds of emotional turmoil inside. These are all components of internal conflict. What happens externally impacts a character on the inside as well. This inside turmoil is called internal conflict.

The kid in the front of the bus notices your pants and starts to laugh. Starting to chant, "Mud pie, Mud pie." Everyone is joining in. This is external conflict. Your reaction on the inside would be internal conflict.

So, you can see that external conflict moves the plot along and internal conflict moves the character's emotional journey along. Both are extremely important. You can't leave one out and have a solid novel. It just isn't possible.

If your character feels shallow with little emotion, you need more internal conflict. If your story is sagging in the middle or moving too slowly, you need more external conflict.

When you write each scene, evaluate the internal and external conflict to be sure that each are present and have some balance. You wouldn't want your character to spend the whole scene thinking. Likewise, you wouldn't want your character to spend a whole scene facing one external conflict after another without any emotional reaction.

**Read the Excerpt Below.** Look for internal and external conflict. Notice it is based on what the character wants.

*Max lifted his crown and stared at his reflection in the mirror. He would never be a brave king like his father. No, he would simply do what he had to. No unnecessary wars. No huge humanitarian cause. Nothing.*

*An emissary of the court fluttered into the room in his journeying cloak. "France has just invaded our southern border. What would you have me to do?"*

*"Call the master of the guard. Tell him to meet me in my chambers."*

*"Yes, your highness."*

*It's inevitable now. King Max sighed and flopped down in the nearest chair. War was coming to him. Like it or not. By the end of the fortnight, he'd be a King of War if he were still king at all.*

## The Internal Conflict:

- Max wants to be a brave king like his father and not feel like a failure.

- Max reflects on his lack of bravery and vision

- Max shows his fear that war will cost him his kingdom

## The External Conflict:

His Dad's Reputation as brave.

The emissary of the court rushing into the room to announce the invasion. In this instance we also have an example of fringe plot conflict. The French come in from the outside and invade the kingdom. This is feasible, but not necessarily seen in the beginning.

## Balance

Now that you understand the difference between external and internal conflict, let's take a look at the importance of balance. A character moves through their world responding to what happens around them and inside of them filtered through their personal goals.

Take the section above. If we took all of the internal conflict out of it, it would read like this:

*Max lifted his crown and stared at his reflection in the mirror.*

*An emissary of the court fluttered into the room in his journeying cloak. "France has just invaded our southern border. What would you have me to do?"*

*"Call the master of the guard. Tell him to meet me in my chambers."*

*"Yes, your highness."*

*King Max sighed and flopped down in the nearest chair.*

This section reads so much different than before. It lacks emotional appeal. I can't seem to get inside the head of King Max at all, accept to know that he is frustrated about something because of his actions at the end.

Now, let's flip it around. Let's remove the external conflict:

*Max lifted his crown and stared at his reflection in the mirror. He would never be a brave king like his father. No, he would simply do what he had to. No unnecessary wars. No huge humanitarian cause. Nothing.*

*It's inevitable now. King Max sighed and flopped down in the nearest chair. War was coming to him. Like it or not. By the end of the fortnight, he'd be a King of War if he were still king at all.*

Once again, we see that something is definitely missing in this passage. We assume this guy is full of himself. He is a whiner and a coward. If we spent much more continuous time in this guy's head, we would be yawning or throwing the book against the wall.

The whole key is balance. Just the right amount of external plot conflict and internal conflict based on the character's personal goals makes for a solid plot line. Your characters will have a stronger spiritual journey and your novel will avoid sagging. Internal and external conflict ideas create the spark that lights our story on fire.

## Practical Application:

Introducing our character, Cara. She is old-fashioned and loves to knit. She is thirty-four and never married. For her thirtieth birthday she moved into an apartment away from her parents. Her goal in this scene is to finish getting ready for her dinner guests before they arrive in thirty minutes.

**What are some possible internal conflicts that could occur in this scene?**

_____

_____

_____

_____

_____

**What are some possible external conflicts that could occur in this scene?**

_____

_____

_____

_____

_____

# Fringe Plotting

Fringe plotting is when something comes from the outside edges of the story to impact your story's plot. It is important that fringe plot is believable and not thrown in at the very end to change the whole story unless it is strongly supported by what you've been building. When you are building the external conflict in your novel, fringe plotting can be a powerful tool. It may cause a conflict in what a character wants for themselves and others.

Some examples of fringe plotting might be an unexpected family tragedy, a great opportunity, the return of an old flame, or a new villain. Anything that comes from the fringes of the story that is believable and creates plot conflict would be an example of fringe plotting.

Let's look again at the story of Cara:

*Cara is old-fashioned and loves to knit. She is thirty-four and never married. For her thirtieth birthday she moved into an apartment away from her parents. Her goal in this scene is to finish getting ready for her dinner guests before they arrive in thirty minutes.*

**What fringe plotting could you do to create some unexpected turns?**

_____

_____

_____

_____

_____

## Pick A Scene From Your Story To Develop.

**Give a basic description of the Point of View Character in your scene.**

_____

_____

_____

_____

**What are the character's goals and stakes in this scene? (What does the character want and why does it matter?)**

_____

_____

_____

_____

**List five possible internal conflicts that could occur in this scene.**

_____

_____

_____

_____

_____

**List five possible external conflicts that could occur in this scene. Make sure two are caused by fringe plotting.**

_____

_____

_____

_____

## Placement of External and Internal Tension

We've covered the difference between external and internal conflict based on what the character wants as well as the importance of balance. It is also important to consider the placement of this conflict throughout the scene. When you light a campfire, you don't strike the flint in the middle of a stand of dry trees or in a snow bank. You don't want to front load all of the internal conflict at the beginning of the scene. Likewise, you don't want to front load all the action and only react to what happens internally at the end. Placing the conflict intermittently will build its impact.

Plot carries the most punch when external and internal conflict are woven throughout the scene. It gives the reader a deeper sense of character POV and makes the stakes more intense.

**Read the following clip:**

_Tammy failed. Nothing else mattered, except getting home before she cried. She would die of embarrassment if anyone saw her. What would they think? She was a loser, no doubt. It wouldn't matter what really happened._

_Tammy bounced up and down on the bus seat. The smell of sweaty bodies and day old peanut butter and jelly sandwiches hung in the_ air. Her friend got off the bus. She waited three more stops before exiting. She finally cried.

This is terrible to read, isn't it? Although it is a short paragraph, we don't really care to read more. The poor placement of internal conflict and external conflict makes this whole paragraph lack any sort of balance and character connection. Let's try this clip again.

*She failed. Nothing else mattered, except getting off the bus before she cried. Tammy bounced up and down on the bus seat. The smell of sweaty bodies and day old peanut butter and jelly sandwiches hung in the air. She sniffled. She would die if anyone saw her.*

*The bus screeched to a stop. Her friend Jenna stood and carried her backpack to the front of the bus. The top of her head disappeared as she walked down the bus steps. She'd been the last friend still on the bus.*

*Tammy flipped the hair out from behind her ear to block her face and stared out the window. Not even summer school could change it. She'd be repeating tenth grade. What would her classmates think? She was a loser, no doubt. She brushed at the moisture that trickled down her cheek.*

*The bus lurched to a stop. She grabbed her backpack off the seat, stepped out into the aisle.*

*Don't let anyone say anything...*

*Tammy pretended to stare past them, the valedictorian, the class bully, all of them. She took a breath.*

*Come on, get a grip.*

*"Have a fun summer," the bus driver said to her back as she bolted down the steps.*

*When her tennis shoes hit gravel, she took off on a dead run. She ran until sobs doubled her over. She'd never survive another year of tenth grade.*

Obviously, here I have extended the story clip quite a bit. But you can see the huge difference it makes to spread the internal and external conflict throughout the scene instead of dumping it all in one place. It carries more emotional punch. Balance plays a huge role in external and internal conflict impact on a scene.

## Practical Application

Caleb has always been sweet on Samantha, the girl next door. He is trying to get up the guts to ask her out. If he fails, he will be embarrassed and have to go to a party alone.

## External Conflict:

- Her dog starts barking at him and Samantha can't hear him over the sound of the barking.

- The phone rings while they are talking.

- Her friend stops by to visit.

- It starts to rain, and he is getting wet on the front step.

## Internal Conflict:

- Caleb has the sudden urge to vomit.

- He is afraid she will turn him down.

- He knows that his friend will ask her out if he doesn't.

- He isn't great at talking when he gets nervous.

Find the points of conflict in your own scene, and list them below using the external and internal conflict points above, or some of your own. Make sure that your scene has a balance of external and internal conflict spread throughout.

_____

_____

_____

_____

_____

_____

_____

_____

_____

_____

_____

_____

_____

Conflict ideas are the metal we strike the flint against to build more meaningful sparks that flame our story. A balance of external and internal conflict creates a deeper character connection in our readers and layers our story to include the spiritual and plot journey of our characters.

Congratulations, you've learned the three components of our fire equation that can help your novel to build and eventually spread like wildfire.

**Flint + Tinder + Metal Friction Sparks = Fire**

**OR**

**Ideas + Character Goals + Stakes + Obstacles = Fire.**

So far, we've covered basic brainstorming strategies, how to identify character goals and stakes, plus how to develop the balance of internal and external conflict in our novels to create sparks. Now, we are ready to dive into some individual brainstorming strategies to find meaningful conflict. These strategies are simple and you will find yourself returning to them time and again as you write your novel, either to eliminate blank page paralysis or just deepen the plot line for your novel.

# PART TWO
## Strategies for Brainstorming Conflict

# Conflict Escalation Strategy

## Mountain Climbing Vs. Plot Plateau

Plot is key to the success of your novel. But so often writers struggle with a sagging middle or what I call a plot plateau in the middle of their novel.

Think of your character as a mountain climber. They start on their journey in Act One and run into the inciting incident (or the event that makes them start on their journey). At this point, they put on their gear and stand looking up at the mountain. It looks steep, they may be afraid of heights, but their long-lost sister is trapped at the top.

They make the decision to climb the mountain. The journey is launched into Act Two. This is where many writers run into all kinds of plot problems. They can set up the story and what the character wants, but they struggle to make the conflict challenges increase in difficulty.

Most writers know to pick out a few conflicts that happen to your character to make it difficult for them to reach the goal. These escalating challenges occur in Act Two and keep the conflict going in the plot. Your character must make decisions to continue on with their journey.

As the climber reaches the first summit, they are struck with fatigue. They want to give up. They must decide whether to continue on to reach the top. They must overcome the roadblock of fatigue to go on. Another two hours up the mountain, they drop their backpack over the edge of the cliff. It has all of their survival supplies inside. Now what? They must once again decide to continue up the mountain. They fall and break their wrist, now it is even more difficult to climb. The pain is excruciating, but they have come so far. They must continue on to find their sister, but they can't go on. The climber believes that she will die on the side of the mountain never having saved her sister.

These crisis situations or conflicts lead the character to their darkest moment and into Act Three. Notice how each of these roadblocks increase in severity. If they leveled out, the conflict would lack punch.

Often, we make the mistake of pulling unrelated conflict into the plot and we wonder why our plot sags. We've been creating conflict that is equal in severity instead of increasing in severity. Our plot has flat lined. We made a plateau and chopped the top right off of the mountain climax that readers are looking for.

A mountain climber doesn't just climb to the summit and circle the mountain on the same level. They reach the summit, catch their second wind and trudge up the side of the mountain straight for the top. The steeper the climb, the more difficult it becomes. Our plots should work the same way.

Each challenge the climber faces is more difficult than the last and begins to work a change in their heart. If your roadblocks are all equal in value, the character will quit growing. For characters to reach the top of the mountain in their spiritual journey, the plot conflict must escalate forcing them to grow.

# Escalating Roadblocks

The first step to avoid the sagging middle is to develop the road-blocks your character will face on their journey and escalate them. You don't want to miss that step or you will find your plot lacking. Here is a simplified example of roadblocks that could happen to a character.

Laura is on the run for her life, all the while she is trying to track down her brother who is missing. Her Roadblocks could be the following:

- She finds a ransom note in her mailbox saying that if she doesn't give them five hundred thousand dollars by tomorrow, she won't see her brother alive again.

- She gets to the bank and they won't loan her the money.

- She tries to sell her families' jewelry, but discovers it isn't worth as much as they had always said.

- A detective steals precious time pulling her down to the precinct to interview her about her brother.

- She finally finds the place her brother is being held. She storms in and finds his bloody clothes all over the place. But no brother. She has failed.

You can see in this plot that the conflict escalates by upping the stakes throughout the story and (for logical flow) by making it harder for her to achieve her goals. Making each roadblock more difficult than the one before builds a mountain, not a plateau.

What if I would have just made the roadblocks equal in size? Like this incident:

She finds the ransom note in her mailbox saying that if she doesn't give them five hundred thousand dollars by tomorrow, she won't see her brother alive again.

- The bank won't loan her money.

- Her father won't loan her money.

- Her bills are overdue and she can't pay them because she is saving all of her money for the ransom.

- She can't meet the deadline, so she approaches the police for help.

- They go with her and find her brother is not there.

Notice that when we get to point four it feels like it is all about the money. It is because we plateau after the bank refuses to lend her money. These challenges are all about equal in intensity. They do not escalate.

In the first example, you see that she tries to borrow money and then she tries to sell the family jewels. This is an escalation of desperation. We feel the building conflict as she holds in her hands the brooch her mother wore and that she is sacrificing it for her brother.

The key to not sagging or hitting a plateau in the middle is all about escalation. There needs to be some point of your plot that is escalating. You can't do everything at once, but there are a variety of places you can escalate your plot conflict to make your characters climb the mountain.

The first way is as I showed you above, escalate the desperation. The character has to give up more and more hoping that at some point it will be enough. It is all about the sacrifice. In example one you see the following escalation:

- She finds the ransom note.

- The bank won't loan her money. She is willing to look bad to save her brother

- She tries to sell family jewels. She is willing to give up something precious to save her brother.

- The detective questions her. She is willing to go against her ethics to hide the truth, which is giving up a core belief practice.

- Her brother isn't there, but blood everywhere. She realizes she can't do this alone.

In this particular example you have an escalation of stakes/desperation. Increasing the desperation or stakes escalates the conflict into a mountain formation.

## Practical Application

Francis is on a wagon train heading west with her husband and young son, Zack. During the first month of the trip, her husband dies of a rattle snake bite. She has to find a way to get herself and Zack safely to Oregon.

Give an example of an escalation in Roadblocks for your character from the plot line.

_____

_____

_____

_____

Look back over what you have written. Is there an escalation of the plot roadblocks for your characters? If not, go back and change things to make it happen.

## Escalating the Threat

Another way to increase the conflict to make a mountain climbing plot is by escalating the threat to your character. This can be an emotional threat, physical threat or a relational threat. All of these are powerful tools and some play better in certain genres than others.

**Example of Escalating the Emotional Threat:**

Bonnie has determined never to fall in love. Her heart has been broken over and over, so when handsome Clay Fallon pulls into town she steers clear of those deep blue eyes that make her knees wobble.

Clay takes a job working for her father on the ranch. Bonnie keeps running into him, and he flirts with her. (She is attracted to him and doesn't want to be.)

Bonnie's father gets hurt in a farming accident, and she has to rely on Clay to help her run the farm while she juggles her already heavy load of chores and nurses her father. (She needs his help, which puts them together more often and her heart begins to soften.)

Clay decides to take her sister to the Fourth of July Dance which makes her realize her true feelings for Clay. (She likes Clay, but she is too late. Her heart is aching.)

Clay seems to have fallen for Bonnie's sister. After all, they spend a lot of time together. And then Bonnie sees them kissing. She doesn't realize that it is her sister surprising Clay with a kiss.

(Bonnie loses the one she loves because she wouldn't open her heart and she got her heart broke in the process.)

## Example of Escalating the Physical Threat:

Ellie has been in the witness protection program for five years since she saw the brutal murder of a known mobster. She gets a letter in the mail addressed to her old name at the current address. It is a warning from a friend back home that someone is out of jail and searching for her. Ellie is determined to keep safe and reclaim her old life, by helping capture her enemy one last time.

- Ellie begins receiving threatening phone calls.

- Ellie is followed in her car by someone from her past who tries to run her off the road.

- Ellie's car is blown up by a bomb meant for her, killing a friend who borrowed it.

- Ellie is kidnapped and the killer holds her till they can find her brother too.

- Ellie believes both of them will die.

## Example of Escalating Relational Threat:

Mark has always loved his wife, but there are some secrets in his past that he has never told her. When a blackmail letter shows up in his email inbox, Mark begins the journey to find and destroy all evidence of his past discretions. **(Threatens break of trust).**

Mark is unable to trace the email to a specific individual, although he thinks he knows who sent it. **(Threatens future of relationship).**

Mark begins to take extra hours after work to track down his enemy. When he keeps saying he has to work late, his wife is beginning to think he is lying to her. **(Threatens destruction of the relationship due to dishonesty).**

The source who sent the email has threatened to go to the press which would ruin his career at a charitable organization. **(Threat to his marriage and career).**

His wife finds out about his past, and it is splashed on the front page news. **(Ultimate devastation when he thinks he will lose everything, including his wife's love).**

## Practical Application

In the boxes below, create an escalating plot line based on the information given.

Tom has always wanted the perfect family life with a picket fence to paint and a wife to call his own. When his fiancé dies in a car accident he believes the dream will never be his, but he searches for a special someone to share his life with. He joins an online Christian dating community and tries to find Ms. Right.

**Give Four Emotional Escalation Roadblocks:**

_____

_____

_____

_____

_____

_____

Tabitha witnesses a drug deal and becomes the target of a drug syndicate. She runs from her family and previous life to escape certain death. Tabitha rushes to identify her enemy before he kills her.

**Give Four Physical Threat Escalations for this story:**

_____

_____

_____

_____

Molly is searching for the daughter she put up for adoption when she was sixteen. She longs to have one last chance to see her daughter before she dies of terminal cancer. This begins her noble quest to find her daughter before she dies.

**Give Four Relational Escalations for this story:**

_____

_____

_____

_____

_____

_____

_____

# Idea Sparking

There are many times we can use the Conflict Escalation Strategy to eliminate the plateaus in our novels and create mountain climbing tension that readers love. Not every area of the story will build exactly the same, but by using a variety of techniques, you will entice readers to stay up late turning pages.

Each point of view character has their own journey. By using the conflict escalation technique at different times for each character, your plot should never plateau, but keep your character climbing mountains.

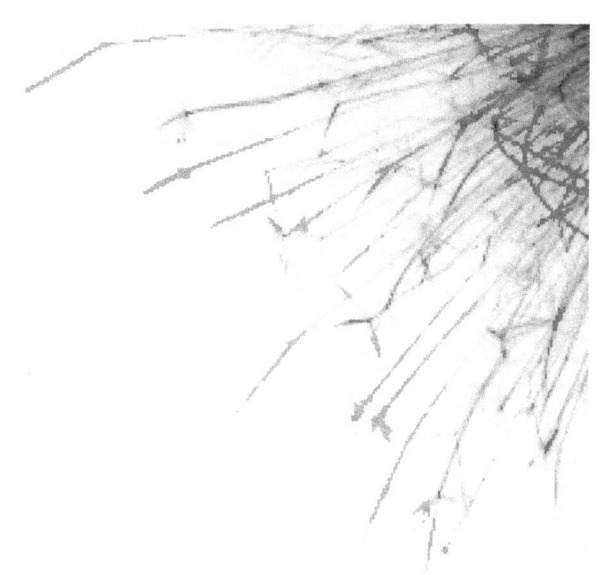

# Boomerang

Although thought to be invented by the Aborigines, boomerangs have morphed into a toy used in several countries of the world. If you look at one you might think what's the big deal? It's just a funny shaped piece of wood or plastic. But once you've tossed one, you just have to see if you can make it *not* return to you.

Why did the boomerang catch on? Because it created an unexpected phenomenon, it returned. You can play it alone, too.

The spread of the boomerang into a variety of cultures should give us a hint that people love the unexpected. So, let's make our plots boomerang.

The moment when you think the boomerang is going one way, it turns around and goes the opposite direction. Right back at you. That is what we need to do with our plots. Avoid the expected outcome of any scene or major plot step, by boomeranging.

Let's start by reading a mini story clip:

*He couldn't have found her. After all these years. Flicked the blinds closed and ran to the closet for her go bag. Her hands trembled as she slid the duffle bag over her shoulder. The thud-thud of her heart in her ears followed the pattern of adrenaline rush. Time to run.*

In this story clip you are set up for a situation where a character could run to hide. Everyone is expecting that to happen. It is still tense, but what if it were more tense than that? Time to boomerang. There are two different ways to boomerang.

## Option One

**Step One:** Answer this question, "What is the most likely thing she will do in this scene?"

**Answer:** Run.

**Step Two:** Think of four alternative things she could do?

**Answers:** Call a friend to come and defend her.

Hotwire her assailant's car after she is sure he has come into the building to get her.

Stay right where she is, because she is tired of running.

Take a gun out of the nightstand to protect herself.

Take her gun out of the nightstand, go down to his car and shoot him.

**Step Three:** Cross out any of the ones above that you have heard done before. If you run out of alternatives, think up some more.

**Narrowed List:** Hotwire her assailant's car after she is sure he has come into the building.

Stay right where she is, tired of running.

Take her gun out of the nightstand, go down and shoot him.

**Step Four:** Eliminate from the list any that are not reasonable for your plot.

**Eliminated List:** Stay right where she is, tired of running. (This is impractical because we don't want our POV character to die.)

Hotwire her assailant's car. (This isn't likely because she would have to know how to do this, and he would be able to trace her car easily if he knows what she is driving).

**Step Five:** Select the best from the remaining list. If the choices aren't strong, start back at step one.

**Best Option:** Take her gun out of the nightstand, go down and shoot him.

Wait one itty bitty minute. Your lead POV character cannot commit murder, right?

**Step Six:** Tweak the best option so that it is feasible to your character.

Basically, we don't want our character to commit murder. Maybe she doesn't kill him. Maybe she just tries to maim him so that he can't come after her for a while. She might even call the paramedics for him, or better yet, calls 911 to report the shooting before she shoots him.

**Final Choice:** She shoots him in the leg in order to escape. When she exits the building, she shoots out his tires to keep him from pursuing her.

Congratulations, you just boomeranged! Notice how opposite your end result is from the beginning where we think she is going to run? Everyone runs, so why should we? We actually ended up doing the opposite. This first boomerang option takes a bit more time, but often gives more creative ideas. You may need to complete the process a few times to come up with the best possible conflict builder. When we create the unexpected, it builds tension in the reader. They just have to know what is going to happen next because they care so much about our character.

## Option Two

Let's look at the clip again.

*He couldn't have found her. After all these years. Destiny flicked closed the blinds and ran to the closet for her go bag. Her hands trembled as she slid the duffle bag over her shoulder. The thud-thud of her heart in her ears followed the pattern of adrenaline rush. Time to run.*

**Step One:** Identify the most common thing a character would do at this point.

**Answer:** Run.

**Step Two:** Write Four Opposite Actions.

**Answers:** Stay.

  Fight.

  Confront.

  Trick/Disguise.

**Step Three:** Pick the most unexpected action, or boomerang. (Usually the opposite)

**Selection:** Confront.

**Step Four:** Develop the action into a complete event.

Confront the assailant with a gun and shoot him in the leg to get away.

Congratulations, you just boomeranged! Both of these options work, it is a matter of personal preference. With the boomerang method, you shouldn't use this too often or your readers will feel like they can predict your unpredictability. Still, it is a good strategy to try when your book is sagging without enough conflict.

## Practical Application

Now it is your turn to try both methods to boomerang a short story clip. Here is the clip:

*The matchmakers were going to make trouble. New Christian bachelor in town and a decent bank account. Dana was surprised the vultures weren't already circling.*

*This time she was at an advantage, she knew he hadn't dated in the year since his girlfriend died in a drunk driving accident.*

**Boomerang Option One**

**Step One:** Answer this question, "What is the most likely thing she will do in this scene?

_____

_____

_____

_____

_____

_____

_____

**Step Two:** Think of four alternate things she could do.

_____

_____

_____

_____

**Step Three:** Cross out any of the ones above that you have heard done before. If you run out of alternatives, think up some more.

_____

_____

_____

_____

**Step Four:** Eliminate from the list any that are not reasonable for your plot.

_____

_____

_____

_____

**Step Five:** Select the best from the remaining list. If the choices aren't strong, start again.

_____

_____

_____

_____

**Step Six:** Tweak the best option so that it is feasible to your character.

_____

_____

_____

_____

## Boomerang Option Two

**Step One:** Identify the most common thing a character would do at this point. (A one-word verb can make this simple as opposed to a longer action phrase.)

_____

_____

_____

_____

**Step Two:** Write Four Opposite Actions.

_____

_____

_____

_____

**Step Three:** Pick the most unexpected action, or boomerang.
(Usually the opposite.)

_____

_____

_____

_____

**Step Four:** Develop the action into a complete event.

_____

_____

_____

_____

_____

_____

Using the boomerang method to increase tension in your novel works because it keeps the reader guessing about what is going to come next. It builds the need to read to find out what will happen on the next page. Like any strategy, be sure to mix it up. No one strategy works all the time. Also, make sure that the boomerang you have picked for your story is feasible.

Sometimes whole novels, or movies are based on this one thing. For example, the movie Ransom is based on a boomerang. When asked for a ransom for his son, the hero said no and turned it back on the kidnapper by offering a reward for his capture. There are many other stories that boomerang as well. It is a helpful strategy to pull out of your bag of tricks when your plot is sagging.

## Let's Review

**Boomerang Method One:**

**Step One:** Answer this question, "What is the most likely thing she will do in this scene?"

**Step Two:** Think of four alternative things she could do.

**Step Three:** Cross out ones you've heard before. Think up alternatves if you run out.

**Step Four:** Eliminate from the list any that are not reasonable for your plot.

**Step Five:** Select the best from the remaining list. If they are too weak, repeat Step One.

**Step Six:** Tweak the best option so that it is feasible for your character.

# Idea Sparking

**Boomerang Method Two:**

**Step One:** Identify the most common thing a character would do in a one-word verb.

**Step Two:** Write four opposite actions in a one-word verb.

**Step Three:** Pick the most unexpected action, or boomerang. (Usually the opposite).

**Step Four:** Develop the action into a complete event.

Do you see how the strategies we've learned so far will help you brainstorm stronger conflict in your novel? You don't have to be a brainstorming guru or even a great plotter to apply the Boomerang Strategy. All you have to do is pick up this book and follow the steps when you are stuck. Now, let's learn some more ways to brainstorm sparks for you novel.

# Mirror Reality

The reflection in the mirror isn't always as kind as we'd like it to be, but it does show us the truth. No hiding those extra pounds, or last week's bad haircut. The mirror tells it like it is, regardless of our feelings.

In our writing we can brainstorm plot conflict by using the concept of mirror reality. Your hero and heroine have disasters waiting to happen in the plot you've created. You can mirror the negative outcome to these disasters to increase the conflict.

Mirror reality is determining a disaster in your character's life that you want to build conflict around. Then have the worst possible outcome of that disaster happen to someone that they know. It will make it feel that much closer to actually happening to them.

**Read the following mini example:**

*If it didn't rain, Reed Duncan would lose it all. The ranch, the cattle, even the house. He kicked his boot at the dirt and watched the swirls of orange dust blow across the range. His whole family would be out in the cold, without a roof over their heads. Reed rubbed at the grit in his eyes. The sun shone with blistering heat. The smell of dirt clogged his throat with a layer of film.*

*"I heard you folks are looking to sell a bit of land on the far side of the river?" Jeb Perkins put a hand on Reed's shoulder and stared across the barren land, hitching his foot on the fence post beside Reed's.*

*"Yep. You interested?" Maybe. Just maybe. Reed pulled his cowboy hat lower to shield his eyes from the sun.*

*"Sorry, got enough to deal with keeping my own land much less anyone else's."*

*"That seems to be the way of it around these parts. Can't half imagine what I'll do if we don't get rain soon."*

In the story clip, you can see that Reed is facing a huge challenge. He is going to lose his ranch if something doesn't change. Then we have a neighbor come on the scene, someone who empathizes with Reed, but doesn't change his situation. Jeb adds a dash of hope before he says that he can't buy the land. This conflict in the scene is small, but does add some tension. There is a stronger conflict option that can be added to this scene to create a more raw character disaster. Let's try adding mirror reality.

By mirroring the worst case scenario in a character's friend or loved one's life we create a whole new spark of conflict. It opens the character to internal conflict over his friend's situation and what might happen to him. The external conflict of the bank sweeping in to take over seems much more real. That is why brainstorming with the Mirror Reality Strategy will increase the conflict options in your novel. So, let's take a look at how it's done.

## Mirror Reality Strategy:

**Step One:** Identify the potential disaster you want to amplify and create more conflict about. This is really important. Not all of the setbacks your character faces are as pivotal to the plot of the story as others. You want to identify one large potential disaster that drives much of the plot to try the mirror reality strategy. This strategy is particularly helpful in building conflict that spreads across the arc of the book. For example, Reed will probably fight this possibility of losing his ranch over the span of several chapters, not just one.

In the story clip, the major disaster we have is the potential for Reed Duncan to lose his ranch. So, that is the potential disaster we should amplify.

**Step Two:** Identify who in the story should experience the disaster. It is best if the mirror reality is applied to someone close to the POV character, someone they respect. That will make it a more real possibility.

In the story clip above, Jeb is a likely candidate; however, if Jeb is important to the story as a mentor for Reed, he may not be your best bet. Another neighbor could be. For this particular story clip, we will use Jeb for our mirror reality character.

**Step Three:** Determine if the mirror reality disaster should happen onstage or offstage. It is always more powerful to have the mirror reality disaster happen in a way that the character directly observes, but occasionally that isn't practical. For example, if your character was on a mission to Mars, it is unlikely that we can have a previous mission's disaster occur on the stage.

In the story clip above, Jeb will have the disaster happen in a way that is evidenced onstage. We could either have him tell his personal experiences to Reed through their discussion, or we can actually have Reed on the scene when the bank takes Jeb's home.

**Step Four:** Create a portion of your hero's/heroine's POV scene that shows the disaster happening to another character. Make this as active as possible. Show the struggle, hurt and tragic results of their worst fears coming true. This POV scene is pivotal to adding internal conflict and bringing the character further along in their spiritual journey.

## Practical Application

Below we have applied the steps learned above for the mirror reality strategy to the story about Reed losing his ranch. As you read the revised clip, look for the following things:

**Step One**: Did we identify and amplify the greatest potential disaster?

**Step Two:** Did we identify who in the story should experience the disaster?

**Step Three:** Did we have the mirror reality disaster happen onstage or offstage?

**Step Four:** Does part of our hero's POV scene show the disaster happening to another character?

**Read the following revised clip:**

*If it didn't rain, Reed Duncan would lose it all. The ranch, the cattle, even the house. He kicked his boot at the dirt and watched the swirls of orange dust blow across the range. His whole family would be out in the cold, without a roof over their heads. He had to think of something. Reed rubbed at the grit in his eyes. The sun shone with blistering heat. The smell of dirt clogged his throat with a layer of film.*

*"I heard you folks are looking to sell a bit of land on the far side of the river?" Jeb Perkins put a hand on Reed's shoulder and stared across the barren land, hitching his foot on the fence post beside Reed's.*

"Yep. You interested?" Maybe. Just maybe. Reed pulled his cowboy hat lower to shield his eyes from the sun.

"Just came over to say good-bye." Jeb shoved his hands in his pocket.

"What?"

"Bank foreclosed on our ranch this morning. Wasn't nothin' I could do about it. I just sat there and watched my Marybelle cry as they boarded up the windows." Jeb swallowed, then continued, his voice thick, "Does somethin' to a man, ya know?"

"Why didn't you say anything?"

Jeb's weathered face wore age in wrinkles like leather. Today he looked older. "What was you going to do? You can't hardly hold on to your own farm."

"We'd have thought of something." Reed gripped the wood fence between scarred knuckles. This couldn't be happening. Not right next door.

"There wasn't nothin' to think of that hadn't been thought of already."

Reed slapped dusty gloves on the fence. "What are you going to do now?"

"We'll head back to Marybelle's family. Her and Samuel can stay with her parents, while I try to find a job and earn enough money to get our own spread again."

Silence fell as they stared at the wind funnels and tumbleweed that disappeared like pipe dreams on the dusty horizon.

"I'm sorry." If things didn't change, Reed would be standing in Jeb's shoes. Reed ran a hand over his face.

*God where are you in all of this?*

*"Me too. I best get back." Jeb turned and stuck out his hand.*

*Reed gripped it in his own, pulling Jeb forward to clap him on the back. "Be sure to tell the missus to write and let us know how y'all are doing."*

*Jeb nodded and turned to walk across the parched dirt. His shoulders sagged with a heaviness Reed could feel settle over his heart.*

*If it could happen to Jeb, it could happen to anyone.*

You can feel the difference in Reed after he experiences his friend's loss. All the things he feared came true for Jeb. Jeb lost his ranch and had to be separated from his family to provide for them and chance the scant possibility that they could buy a new spread.

By mirroring the disaster that Reed is trying to avoid in another character, we have made the possibility seem so much greater and thus created stronger conflict. This strategy can be very effective if used with the right disaster, character, and placement in the story. If we put this scene right at the end of the book, the conflict from this isn't drawn out for as long. You can build on Jeb's story through the heroine's point of view as well. Maybe she is friends with Marybelle.

## Heroine's POV Mirror Reality

**Step One:** Identify and amplify the greatest potential disaster for your heroine. For our heroine, we'll call her Lily for now, the greatest disaster might be the splitting up of the family. Remember, not all parts of a conflict will affect each POV character the same. Women tend to be more relational and Lily might be more upset about losing the family than the farm.

**Step Two:** Identify who in the story should experience the disaster or mirror reality. In this case we already have Marybelle as experiencing the loss of her farm and her family being split up while her husband finds work. She should be a good friend of Lily's, maybe even a woman she views as having it all together and a great homemaker. This will build the fear that if Marybelle can't do this, how can she?

**Step Three:** Determine if the mirror reality disaster should happen onstage or offstage. It might be most powerful if Lily saw Marybelle have her possessions stripped away from her, but since Reed already has acknowledged that they were unaware of the situation we will put it at Lily's house.

**Step Four:** Create a scene in our heroine's POV that shows the disaster happening to another character. Remember, the most powerful mirror reality candidates are ones close to the hero/heroine.

**Below is a small clip of what the scene in Lily's POV might look like:**

*How much did she really have to eat to keep the baby healthy? Lily rested a hand over her belly and peered down into the pot of beans. The smell of bacon grease made her stomach churn with morning sickness. So far, she'd hid it from Reed, but it wouldn't be long before that was impossible.*

*"How far along are ya?" Marybelle put the dipper into the water bucket and lifted it to her lips.*

*"About two months I reckon. Don't tell Reed. He's got enough to worry about."*

*Marybelle's eyes teared up. She sniffed and turned away. "Reckon so." The sound was strangled and weak.*

*"Oh, Marybelle." Lily threw her arms around her friend. "I'm sorry. Here I am carrying on and you've lost your farm."*

*Marybelle pulled away and dabbed at the corner of her eyes with her apron. "It's not the farm I'll miss the most."*

*"What are you going to do?" What are we going to do? The questions ran together with no good answer. Not one she could live with.*

*"We're headed back to my folks. Jeb will try to get work and send money. It's like my whole family is splitting apart." Marybelle's shoulders caved forward and shook with sobs.*

*"Shh. It'll all work out, you'll see." Lily rubbed a hand up and down her back. She told herself the same thing every night, but she still didn't believe it. Marybelle's family was ripping apart; what if hers was next?*

Do you see how mirroring Lily's fears in Marybelle's life can be powerful? We see the devastation that can occur if Lily's worst fear comes true through Marybelle's experience. We see the uncertainty Lily is feeling about her own future. Without this scene in the novel, the disaster has less punch, less conflict opportunity. This is an additional layer of conflict building action that you can do with one simple strategy.

## Practical Application:

Now it is your turn. Follow the mirror reality strategy steps to create greater tension in one of your scenes.

**Step One:** Identify the potential disaster you want to create more tension around and amplify it.

_____

_____

_____

_____

**Step Two:** Identify who in the story should experience the disaster.

_____

_____

_____

_____

**Step Three:** Determine if the mirror reality disaster should happen onstage or offstage.

_____

_____

_____

_____

**Step Four:** Create a portion of your hero's/heroine's POV scene that shows the disaster happening to another character.

_____

_____

_____

_____

_____

_____

# Idea Sparking

## Let's Review The Mirror Reality Strategy:

**Step One:** Identify the potential disaster you want to amplify and create more conflict about.

**Step Two:** Identify who in the story should experience the disaster.

**Step Three:** Determine if the mirror reality disaster should happen onstage or offstage.

**Step Four:** Create a portion of your hero's/heroine's POV scene that shows the disaster happening to another character.

Mirror Reality is just one more strategy that can be used to build the conflict in our fire equation. If you apply it to your novel you will have an overarching conflict that weaves through the whole novel.

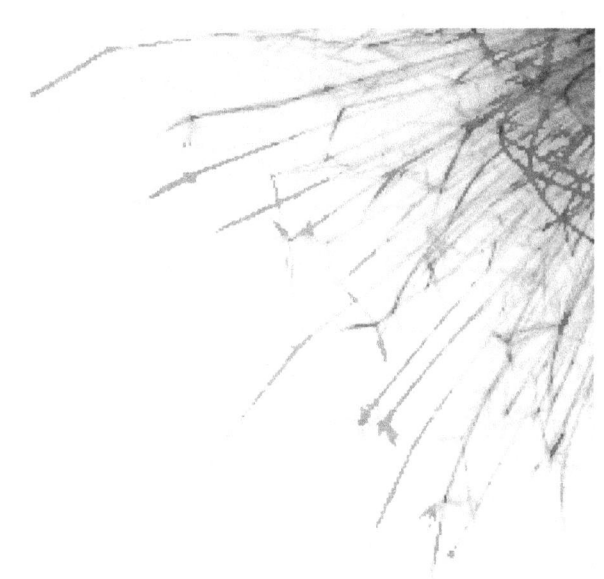

# Pedestal Principles

New Year's resolutions are a practice many of us do every year, but very few of us actually reach our goals. Sometimes it is because we aren't as disciplined as we hoped we would be and other times we set unrealistic goals that are almost impossible to attain.

If you haven't exercised even once a week all year the previous year, it isn't very likely that you will exercise every day this year. That would probably be an unrealistic goal beyond what you can reasonably attain.

We set ourselves up for unrealistic goals when we are very disappointed in where we are right now. Our characters do the same thing. They set themselves up for unrealistic goals because they don't like where they are in life at the moment. We can use these unrealistic goals to cause all kinds of conflict.

**Some examples of unrealistic character expectations:**

- Avoiding men altogether because they cause heartache. (This would be unrealistic for a heroine who is an executive in charge of quality control on an oil rig. A lot of male workers in this field.)

- Catching a killer before anyone else dies. (The pattern says he will kill again in one day, and the hero has no information that would lead to his identity yet.)

- Not giving in to the truth serum. (By its very nature, truth serum takes over and doesn't allow the POV character to resist).

- Raising $10,000,000 toward a charity. (The POV character's only experience with fund raisers is selling candy bars.)

Personal pedestal principles are the unrealistic expectations we have for ourselves or the unrealistic expectations other have of us. These unrealistic expectations, or Pedestal Principles can create conflict in one scene or across the whole plot of the novel, depending upon what it is. Characters have unrealistic expectations of themselves all the time, just like us. When we remember to include them, it makes our characters feel more human. Pedestal principles work best at stirring up internal conflict because they are in direct relationship to what we believe. When the POV Character's values come into conflict with unrealistic expectations, inner turmoil results.

What is a character value? Values are the things that are most important to your character. Some value courage, others independence, still others, loyalty. It is the culmination of the beliefs and experiences you grew up with. If I grew up in a controlling home, then I might value independence more than most. A character's values are the things they believe to be important.

Pedestal Principles come into conflict with our values when they are at odds. In the chapter's examples you will get a better idea of how these values can play against unrealistic expectations we have of ourselves.

How about the expectations of our loved ones, or a boss at work? They often have expectations of us that are almost beyond reach and they are experts at piling pressure on top of these pedestal principles. It serves as a pressure cooker as we try to juggle the demands of everyone in our lives, including ourselves.

**Some examples of unrealistic expectations from our character's connections:**

- A mom who expects her surgeon daughter to make every family event even if it means missing an emergency page.

- A boss who expects his employee to finish a major project in twenty-four hours that would normally take two weeks.

Overwhelming expectations create conflict in our character's journey. Some expectations are difficult to achieve, others next to impossible. By revealing these high expectations or what I call pedestal principles we open our character to a whole new level of conflict.

Pedestal principals build the pressure your character faces when they go against the core values of the character. Because the character must choose between a core value and an unrealistic expectation, it often ups the tension in your novel.

There are two different places that this pressure can come from in our character's life. Let's brainstorm them both.

**Step One:** Determine the core values of your character.

For Example: Kate is a speech clinician. She values loyalty, kindness, sensitivity to those less fortunate, and managing her time to help as many people as possible.

**Step Two:** Use these core values and build a list of possible pedestal principles. Here are some possibilities for this example:

- Helping as many kids in her job as possible, not letting anyone slip through the cracks.

- Challenging a teacher to change their instructional habits to better help a student.

**Step Three:** Create a situation that opposes these principles

She is forced to choose between loyalty to someone she cares about and her values. Being sensitive to others increases her workload because she doesn't want to inconvenience others.

**Step Four:** Integrate these pedestal principles into the plot of the book to build tension.

**Read the following mini story clip:**

*If she didn't get out of here soon, she'd be a sitting duck in a dark parking lot. Kate still needed to update the assessment file on one of her students before driving home. She looked at the clock on the wall over her desk. The hiss of the wall heater echoed in the empty office. Stalker or not, she wasn't about to sacrifice the important things for a moron who took photos and left presents on her doorstep.*

Go back and review the pedestal principles we built above the story clip. Do you see how we integrated those principles into the plot of the story clip? Normally, this scene would be tense because Kate is walking to her car in the parking lot by herself and we know she has a stalker. Adding the conflict that makes her stay late to walk the parking lot in the dark creates a conflict buildup. We are all shouting....No, leave now. We can feel the stage being set. In this instance, taking advantage of her pedestal principles comes in handy.

## Pedestal Principles Established By Others

The previous example focused on the set of pedestal principles we took from our heroine herself. Now let's take a look at secondary characters who create a pressure cooker in the lives of our characters. These people can be anyone in the cast of characters that your hero/heroine care about or are in authority over your character. The more your character cares about the person who is imposing their values on the character's life, the more power these pedestal principles will have over their actions.

Who might some of these people be? Family, employers, church communities, business partners, etc. The closer they are to the character, the more intense the character's response will be to their influence.

**Let's look at the example of Elliot:**

**Step One:** Write the core values of your character below.

For Example: Elliot values quality, family, adventure, responsibility.

**Step Two:** Use these core values and build a list of possible Pedestal Principles.

- Elliot wants to produce quality work at his job.

- Elliot loves to take adventurous family vacations.

- Elliot believes you should be there for your family when they need you.

**Step Three:** Create a situation with another person that opposes these principles.

- Elliot's boss is all about quantity. The more you get done the better. This forces Elliot to produce quality work in less time.

- Elliot's wife likes stability. She doesn't prefer to take risks or go on adventures.

- Elliot's daughter has leukemia. He has to miss a lot of work to be there for her treatment, yet he doesn't want to lose his job or do poorly at his job.

(In this last one, you can see two of Elliot's core values pitted against each other, and he must decide what is more important. That creates even more tension.)

**Step Four:** Add the pedestal principles strategy into your story.

**Read this mini story clip:**

*Camy's hat covered a balding head, but it couldn't hide the gray pallor of her skin, or the tinge of blue around her lips. Elliot watched the fading sunlight filter through the window and land on the comforter that stretched over his daughter's frail body.*

*Cancer had ravaged them all.*

*Elliot ran a hand over his face. He had to leave for work again. If he didn't keep his job, there would be no health insurance, no money for treatment. How could he leave knowing that her last breath might be without him here?*

*Camy's small hand reached across the covers to squeeze his calloused one that rested on his knee. She was saying it was okay. She was braver than Elliot would ever be.*

*"I love you, baby." Elliot stood and brushed a kiss across her fore-head. "I'll see you tonight." He had to. A world without Camy...*

In this story clip, Elliot was forced to choose between staying with his daughter or going to work to raise money for her treatment. He doesn't know how much longer she will live. You feel his conflicted emotions, his angst. Two of his core values war with each other in a pressure cooker. Applying the Pedestal Principles Strategy we upped the conflict and inner turmoil for our character. This again can be an overarching conflict that carries the distance of a book, or it can be something you use in one scene only.

This strategy is best used on internal conflict, building up the inner angst of your character when they can't reach the expectations set for them. However, you can also build the external conflict by having other characters turn up the conflict with their actions in the scene by opposing what the hero/heroine wants. Building both the internal and external conflict at the same time packs the most punch.

## Practical Application

Now it is your turn to try adding pedestal principals to one of your scenes to build tension. Choose a scene that is falling a bit flat and has room in it for a values war.

**Strategy One:** What are your character's core values?

_____

_____

_____

**Based on these core values, make a list of pedestal principles.**

_____

_____

_____

_____

**Create a situation that opposes these principles.**

_____

_____

_____

_____

Make sure to apply these techniques to scenes from your own manuscript. In what scenes from your novel could you integrate one of these pedestal principles to build tension?

**Strategy Two:** List some characters that could be in opposition to your main character's core values to add pedestal principle pressure.

_____

_____

_____

_____

**What are your character's core values?**

_____

_____

_____

_____

**Based on these core values, make a list of pedestal principles.**

_____

_____

_____

_____


**Create a situation that opposes these principles.**

_____

_____

_____

_____


What scenes from your novel could you rewrite to include tension from other characters' pedestal principles?

# Idea Sparking

## Let's Review

### Pedestal Principles Type One:

(Built from the characters expectations of themselves.)

**Step One:** Determine the core values of your character.

**Step Two:** Use these core values and build a list of possible pedestal principles.

**Step Three:** Create a situation that opposes these principles.

**Step Four:** Integrate these pedestal principles into the plot of the book to build tension.

### Pedestal Principles Type 2:

(Built from the expectations others place on the character.)

**Step One:** Identify some of the cast that could impose pedestal principles on your character.

**Step Two:** Write the core values of your character below.

**Step Three:** Use these core values and build a list of possible pedestal principles.

**Step Four**: Create a situation that opposes these principles.

**Step Five:** Add the pedestal principles strategy into your story.

Using the Pedestal Principle Strategy can bring conflict to individual scenes and the whole novel. They stir up internal conflict best, but they also have some potential to create external conflict between the hero/heroine and the character who interferes with the core value of the character.

# Secret Sabotage

Did you know there is a website on secrets where you can post your secret and get advice anonymously? That raises all kinds of questions for me about people. The biggest one being, if it's anonymous, how do you know if the advice is any good? I guess I'd just as soon tell my friend as an online entity that I don't know, but not everyone is the same way.

Tabloids thrive on discovering the secrets of the rich and famous element of our society. And if we didn't care, that would put them out of business. Still, the masses tune in by the thousands to hear the tell-all stories of killers, actors, actresses, presidents, politicians, and more.

Secrets are big news, so what can we as writers do to add secret sabotage as a conflict building strategy in our novels? It's easier than you think. But as always we will start with brainstorming.

**Step One:** Brainstorm a list of each character and what would be embarrassing to them.

**Dana-** would be embarrassed if people knew she was a pro-abortion demonstrator in her college days because now she is pro-life.

**Will-** would be embarrassed if people knew that he had a DUI ten years ago.

**Liz-** would be embarrassed if people knew that she gambled away all her money and now she has poor credit because she took out loans to cover her gambling debts.

**Jeremy-** would be embarrassed if anyone new that he never finished high school.

**Step Two**: Brainstorm a situation where that information could come out.

**Dana-** A fellow demonstrator friend from college is in town to visit family.

**Will-** He gets arrested for speeding, or is being questioned in regards to a hit and run.

**Liz-** If she tried to apply for a car or house loan. Any situation where her credit would be checked.

**Jeremy-** If he applied for a position at any job or any volunteer place that required work history or resume.

**Step Three**: Brainstorm how hiding this secret could make them do something unexpected or out of character to hide it.

Dana is up for an administrator position at a pro-life adoption agency in town. Her college friend Jill comes back to visit her family. She calls to see if Dana wants to get together with her. Dana avoids her, says she's busy. She is afraid if they get together and other people run into them, that the information will get out.

Will is being investigated for a hit and run in the neighborhood. He packs his bags and skips town just before a major opportunity for him to display his artwork. Normally, he would never leave, but his secret creates an unexpected action.

Liz is offered a board position at a very prestigious nonprofit corporation. She turns it down surprising everyone around her, because it is something she has always wanted. She discovered that they would have to run a credit check before hiring her. She doesn't want to lose face in the community, so she turns it down.

Jeremy never applies for higher end jobs even when the opportunity presents itself to work in his girlfriend's employer's company. He knows that he will never get the job without a high school diploma, but he doesn't want his girlfriend to know about it. This creates a lot of tension opportunities between them.

**Step Four**: Brainstorm a list of people who may know the secret, tell or threaten to tell it.

**Dana-** Her college friend might threaten to tell if she doesn't give her a recommendation for a job at Dana's company. The other person who wants the position may know and threaten to squeal if she applies for the job she wants.

**Will-** The sherriff and his older sister, who have thier eyes on the family land. She tries to claim the land after the will is read saying her parents were not competent to sign a new will. She threatens that if he fights, she will send a letter to his current employer telling of his criminal status.

**Jeremy-** His brother is a teacher at the high school, so he often encourages Jeremy to come for GED classes. His employer might take advantage of him because he knows that he can't get a better job.

**Step Five**: Write a scene that illustrates the threat to show secret sabotage.

## Example Brainstorm

For this purpose we will use the character Liz. Here were her brainstorm steps again:

**Step One:** (Brainstorm what would embarrass your character): Liz would be embarrassed if people knew that she gambled away all her money and now she has poor credit because she took out loans to cover her gambling debts.

**Step Two:** (How could it be revealed?) Liz tried to apply for a car or house loan. Any situation where her credit would be checked.

**Step Three**: Liz is offered a board position at a very prestigious nonprofit corporation. She turns the position down surprising everyone around her, because it is her dream job. She discovers they will run a credit check before hiring her. She doesn't want to lose face in the community, so she turns it down.

**Step Four:** (Who might threaten to expose your character?) The banker whose kid was in her Sunday School class and she caught him smoking marijuana at church. Tells her to keep her mouth shut or he will revoke her loan.

**Step Five:** (Create a scene that illustrates the threat.)

*Smoking pot on church grounds was no small thing. Liz pressed the wrinkles from her Sunday dress. A thick coating of sweat dotted her upper lip. "Mr. Brandt. I wanted to discuss something with you, before taking any further action."*

*Mr. Brandt pulled his pocket watch out of his three-piece suit coat pocket. Tie and a tight white collar framed his red face and jowls. "Whatever it is, I'm quite certain that Dillon will apologize and refrain from such behavior in the future." He scowled at his teenage son, who sat across from Liz in bad boy rags and a nose piercing.*

*"I think it will take a bit more action on your part, sir." Liz folded and unfolded her hands three times. There had to be a way to get him to see reason. "Dillon was smoking pot in the boiler room."*

*"Is that what is this all about? Smoking weed?" Mr. Brandt placed a pudgy hand on the Sunday School room table. "Dillon, wait outside."*

Dillon's I-told-you-so smirk mocked her as he slunk out of the room tugging at the corner of his jeans, which barely covered his boxers. The faint smell of marijuana followed him from the room.

"Look, Mr. Brandt. This is the third time this month. I think your son has a drug problem. It's time you got him some help." Liz's pulse pounded in her ears.

"No, Mrs. Haneman. You look! My son is in that experimental stage of his teen years. You have no right to tell me how to raise my son." His stale breath blew in her face.

"If you won't get him help, I will—"

"You so much as breathe a word of this to anyone, and I'll see to it that everyone knows about your little gambling problem. You got that?" He jabbed his finger in front of her nose.

"Don't you forget it." Mr. Brandt stood and yanked his rain slicker off of the back of the folding chair. The air whooshed behind him as he slammed the door.

If she didn't tell someone about Dillon's addiction, he would likely ruin his life. If she did, she'd likely ruin hers.

Do you see how we used Liz's values to play against one another and create a decision point in the novel? Huge conflict is infused into the book when we add the strategy of Secret Sabotage. Feeding off of this could be her denial to testify in court as requested by her romantic interest to get Dillon placed in a treatment facility. You can keep feeding on this conflict throughout a major portion of the book, each time escalating the conflict.

## Practical Application

Secret sabotage is a very successful technique as long as you remember to use step three and have your character do some confusing things as a result of a secret they don't want to come out. It builds conflict and confusion in the cast that adds depth to your plot. Build the threat scene into the mix and now you have intense conflict, both externally and internally. Now it's your turn to give it a try.

**Step One**: List your characters and something that would embarrass them.

_____

_____

_____

_____

**Step Two**: Brainstorm a situation where that information could come out.

_____

_____

_____

_____

**Step Three**: Brainstorm how hiding this secret could make them do something unexpected or out of character to hide it.

_____

_____

_____

_____

**Step Four**: Brainstorm a list of people who may know the secret, tell or threaten to tell it.

_____

_____

_____

_____

**Step Five**: Create a scene that illustrates the threat.

_____

_____

_____

_____

# Idea Sparking

## Let's Review

**Secret Sabotage Strategy:**

**Step One**: Brainstorm a list of what would embarrass each of your characters.

**Step Two**: Brainstorm a situation where that information could come out.

**Step Three**: Brainstorm how hiding this secret could make them do something unexpected or out of character to hide it.

**Step Four**: Brainstorm a list of people who may know the secret, tell or threaten to tell it.

**Step Five**: Write a scene that illustrates the threat to show secret sabotage.

Utilizing the Secret Sabotage Strategy you can pit a character's secrets against the consequences of telling the truth. This strategy can be used throughout the whole book, or just in a scene. Make sure to create unexpected behavior from your character that comes from this secret adding an element of surprise to your plot.

# Villain Scouting

Remember that girl in high school that caused everyone trouble? She taunted, told our secrets and embarrassed us all to elevate her own position. She made people's lives miserable, but boy could she turn on the charm when the "right" people were around. She is a villain in the story of our lives.

Often when we come up with villains, we assume they are the creepy guys lurking in the corner or the vindictive black widow, but there are other types of villains who are valuable to all genres, not just suspense. A villain is simply someone who goes against our goals and makes life difficult. They are not all the same type, nor do they embody the same danger, but all of us should have someone who opposes our character's views in a book. Let's look at a few different kinds of villains.

## Double-faced villains

These are the villains like the girl in high school who can turn on the sweet innocent girl with the snap of a finger, but she can be vicious and cause all kinds of trouble for our characters.

**Read the following story clip:**

*Destiny brushed her blood red nails against her jacket and then blew at them. "He'll never like you. He doesn't date ugly."*

Samantha swallowed back the tears that clogged her throat. "You can't fool him forever. He'll eventually figure out what a witch you are."

"Like that will ever happen." Destiny's shift from bitter to charm transformed her face. She flipped her blonde hair off her shoulder and pasted on her Colgate grin. "Mark," sweet dripped off the word, "I can't wait till the dance."

Samantha looked over her shoulder to encounter the warmest chocolate brown eyes and cutest dimples. Mark.

Destiny linked her arms through Mark's, looked up into his handsome face, and blinked.

From this clip you get a sense of this two-faced character. Remember, they can also be older or be a guy. Think about your life and the villain types you've run into that are two-faced. How about the oily car salesman? This is one type of villain who often works well in romances, but you can use this character in a variety of genres.

## Blackmail Villain

This villain is a secret broker. He or she uses the information gleaned from the town gossip to further their agenda. They use secrets to get people to do what they want and sometimes just to exert their power. There is a huge rush in having the upper hand and they thrive on it. You aren't afraid of them in a dark alley. Chances are the blackmail villain is well-liked and suave, but the hero's/heroine's real fear of them is the danger the villain poses to a relationship with someone the hero/heroine loves. Someone who doesn't know their secrets.

**Read the following story excerpt:**

He was done with it. After today, Daniel could do his own dirty work. Cameron held the flashlight over the file cabinet and flipped through *the files. If Cameron hadn't screwed up, he wouldn't be here at three a.m. digging for the will.*

*He pulled a piece of paper free from a file, folded it and crammed it in his jean pocket. He slid the drawer closed and slipped out of the office and down the dark corridor. His cell phone vibrated against his hip. He pulled it out of its holster and stared at the number, flipping it open he held it to his ear. "What?" He hissed scurrying toward the security exit.*

*"You're late. I thought you understood the timetable. I'd hate for your wife to find photos in your mailbox."*

*"I got it. I'll be there in ten." Cameron flipped the phone closed. Tonight was the last time. The lies had gotten too thick to navigate.*

The blackmail villain typically goes for the heart of the things we value. In this case, Cameron values his marriage. He is willing to do things he normally wouldn't do, to keep his indiscretion a secret. This is the kind of villain that allows us to bring out unexpected behavior in our characters for the secrets they keep.

## High Concept Villain

This particular villain is often underused. The concept villain causes conflict and difficulty in our lives by its existence. Things like war, fighting over peace, values, causes, lack of faith, heroic jobs, etc. This is stuff that is thrown into the mix to create trouble for our characters because of the conflict they represent. Wars keep people apart. Heroic jobs require difficult hours and a high level of danger that puts additional stress on families. Someone's lack of faith may keep us apart. An old family feud based on political views in the south can derail a romantic relationship.

**Read the following story clip:**

*"I do declare, Mary. You have the oddest taste in men. May hap you didn't know he's a Yankee born and bred not five miles from our plantation." Suzanna fluttered her fan against the thick July humidity.*

*The front porch shade did little to keep Mary cool in the heavy petticoats mama insisted upon. She stamped her foot against the white porch floorboards. "Tis none of your business who I set my cap for, Suzanna. If you weren't so particular, maybe you wouldn't be the oldest unmarried chit in these parts."*

*Suzanna gasped, "Well, I never—"*

*"Face it. With all the men off to war, 'tis slim pickings. At least he's easy on the eyes."*

In this scene the war and the different political views of the time become a villain. They interfere with dating and being allowed to court someone with opposing views. These are high concept villains who impact the whole story, but don't show up in bodily form.

## Good Intentions Villain

These are family members and caring individuals that attempt to do what they believe is best for for the character, but actually it plays the roll of the villain in the character's life. She match makes and invites both character to dinner, but they don't realize it until they get there. It is unexpected conflict for the hero/heroine, but the villain isn't trying to hurt them.

**Read the following story clip:**

*A rosie-cheeked Audrey opened the door to greet Beth. The smell of lasagna wafted from the kitchen and made her stomach grumble.*

*"I'm so glad you made it. I was beginning to worry you got cold feet."*

*"Didn't figure that would do much good. You'd have been a'knocking on my door."*

*"That is one of the advantages of living next door. Can keep my eye on you and make sure you're okay."*

*"Let's just get this over with." Beth stepped inside the living room filled with antiques from the high back chair to the lamp that rested on the coffee table. All a picture of yesterday in floral patterns. If only Audrey hadn't filled her emptiness after her husband's passing by finding romance for each single girl at Lakeside Community Church. She followed the rug floor runner to the end of the hall and turned to walk into the dining room, stopping short of the table.*

*Four familiar faces sat around the table, all looking at her now that she came in. Since when did Audrey plan for a double date? And what was Seth doing here... with someone else? Beth swallowed the disappointment that clogged her throat. Just get through tonight! She gripped the empty chair in her hands and pulled it out. She sat down and stared at the delicate china pattern that lined the plate. Anywhere, but the set of chocolate eyes that burned its gaze on the top of her head. Boy did Audrey miss the mark this time.*

In this scene, Audrey has good intentions, but through her meddling, she has made things worse for Beth. Beth has to be on a blind date with a guy from church in front of the guy she really likes. Talk about tension. This deepens the plot. Sometimes the three-way love triangle in books gets old. You know, where the woman has to choose between two guys. Some readers don't like that, but this allows that same kind of tension without creating dual relationships for the heroine. Just dual conflicts of dating situations.

## Reluctant Villain

This is the villain who does bad things because they feel they have no choice. They will lose something or someone they love if they don't comply. It is the villain who shows up to rob a bank just to have enough money to pay ransom for the little girl that is held hostage. These villains are people we often trust because in real life they are kind, family-centered individuals with a great record in the community. Their personal values are attacked by a greater need to protect and care for those in their lives.

**Read the following story clip:**

*A life in prison was nothing next to the alternative. Jake pressed his back into the brick face of the building. The moonlight reflected off the puddles along the dark alley. The steam from a vent spewed gray puffs of cloud covering the dumpster a hundred feet away. He breathed in and out. Pressed his hand against his chest that throbbed with rapid beats.*

*The door opened down the alley. He tightened his grip on the pipe. He just needed the information hidden in her bag. No one had to die. Jake covered the distance between them with as little sound as possible. He lifted the pipe. God forgive him.*

As you can see, this villain is remorseful. He doesn't delight in what he is doing, he just wants to get it over with. You can feel it in the words he uses. A villain like this will also try to hide what it is they are covering. For example, if he has to bring back information in exchange for his family's life, he is likely to try to hide that anything is wrong. He won't want additional attention drawn to him, because it could put his family in danger. You can use the secret in this situation to a additional conflict in several scenes. These scenes can bring actions that are confusing to your other POV characters.

## Revenge Villain

The revenge villain is trying to get even for something that has happened to them, or someone they love. They are unable to forgive and the hatred burns in them and dictates their actions. This person will seem jaded or angry sometimes. They may have difficulty with close relationships because they can't let go of the past. Women often fit in this role very well. People don't assume that female characters are capable of this kind of hatred and they pity her for what she has been through. This often gets her off the hook for poor behavior and fuels the growing monster in her soul.

**Read the following story clip:**

*He'd get what he deserved, even if it cost her everything. Daphne stared at the picture of the man who'd unraveled her life. So cocky, and suave. No one knew what he was really like. Except Daphne.*

*The hum of the heater filled the stillness of the political campaign office. Everyone had gone home, but her. Daphne leaned back in her chair and stared at the campaign paraphernalia in red, white, and blue.. as if he could put his country or anything else before himself. She'd be the dutiful little campaign manager for now, until the time was right.*

You notice that in this clip I spent quite a bit of time in the villain's head. My purpose was to give you a look at the inside of the revenge villain's mind. This kind of villain can be very powerful, especially if their anger is aimed at your hero, heroine, or their loved ones. This villain is a great parallel to the spiritual truth of forgiveness. Sometimes you show the opposite, so a hero/heroine can see where they will be if they don't forgive. This villain works great for that.

## Physical Villains

A physical villain is something that attacks the hero/heroine, like: cancer, a virus outbreak, personal disability, or some sort of physical illness or wound that attacks them. The physical villain plays havoc with the hero's/heroine's life life by affecting health, finances, and strength. This villain is often used in conjunction with another one, or in novels that are in a less suspenseful genre. You want adversity for your characters, so bring this kind of villain to up the tension.

**Read the following story clip:**

*Hemorrhaging on patient zero started five minutes ago. Dr. Kathy Lathum stood surrounded by a crowded ward of sick patients. It would get worse before it got better. Time to call in the CDC. This was no ordinary virus, and she'd been exposed. No weekend at the lake with Christy, or sailing with the handsome neighbor down the street.*

*Kathy brushed a stray hair back from her face with an elbow. Her face mask and blue scrubs were hardly enough protection. "Nurse, I'm going to the decontamination room. Put all the staff on alert. We need to set up quarantine and follow infectious disease protocol."*

*"Yes, Doctor." The wide-eyed twenty-something nurse scurried from the room.*

*Kathy watched her leave, then turned to stare down at the ravaged face of patient zero... her patient zero. Her high school sweetheart Caleb Brennan.*

In this scene alone we have layered in a few different conflicts with the physical villain, or in this case, the virus. So, the doctor is facing a virus that requires the CDC, patient zero is hemorrhaging, patient zero is an old sweetheart, the Dr. has been exposed to the disease, and it is alluded at that the young nurse she is working with has too. Additionally, we see it will mean not spending time with family and having to trust someone who wasn't very experienced, the young nurse. The physical villain allows for tons of conflict both personally and professionally, plus it carries societal conflict as well.

## Dark & Twisted Villain

The dark and twisted villain seems to be the one we are most acquainted with in novels and on television. But sometimes we apply the dark twisted villain thought pattern to other types of villains where it doesn't belong. The dark and twisted villain is evil. They are mentally or emotionally deficient. This group includes psychopaths, sociopaths and other mentally ill characters. The dark and twisted villain does reprehensible things that we can't even begin to comprehend. This type of villain usually is in a suspense or thriller.

Darkness pervades the way they think and behave. Oftentimes people don't even realize that they are evil. They are suave, sophisticated, intelligent and good looking. They have snowed lots of people, but in the core they are evil. They often are arrogant and look down on other people as if they are inferior. There are many variations of this villain. It is advantageous to look at FBI profiles for these types of criminals, so you can create a believable one.

**Read the following story clip:**

*The darkness settled like a blanket smothering light from the horizon. Colby idled in the shadows near the park entrance and waited for his prey. Trees lined the running path, stretching shadows with moon glow. It was time for her to die.*

*Colby opened the car door and climbed out. The humid air clung to his black leather jacket and pasted his hair to his head. He closed the door and slid on his leather gloves. Soon she would know to fear him. Stupid woman was a creature of habit. Now she was his for the kill. He walked several yards along the tree line out of sight of the street. He would wait here. The smell of earth, like a cemetery, clung to the night. The slap of sneakers on tar. Adrenaline sluiced in his veins. It was time.*

Notice that with the dark and twisted villain you see arrogance and darkness. Premeditation and stalking are big elements for this type of villain. They also like trophies and reflecting on their evil. This behavior adds a dark element to the villain when we get inside their head. We can show them interacting with the people around them who are totally unaware of their evil side. We can even keep the identity of the killer unknown to our reader for awhile. This villain should give our readers the chills and make them want to stand up for all that is right.

## Overview

There are several different kinds of villains. Not all of the personality types are in this chapter, but you do see several of the most common ones. If you write suspense, you already know that there has to be a villain in your story. But to deepen your novel whether you are a suspense writer or not, adding a villain is a powerful way to escalate the conflict and unexpected turns in your story.

## Practical Application

Pick three kinds of villains to develop as possibilities for your own story. You won't use them all, but brainstorming at least three varieties will give you more choices and help you find the best conflict and plot villain for your novel.

**Three Villain Types I Plan To Develop For My Story Are:**

_____

_____

_____

**Make sure to brainstorm each of your villains.** The following questions are a guide to what would be helpful to brainstorm for story use.

- How does my villain cause trouble for my hero/heroine?

- What sort of wicked habits does my villain have?

- Why is the villain out to get my character?

- Does anyone suspect my character's evil?

- What motivates my villain or what has made them who they are?

- What does s/he think about?

- What are their hobbies?

- What annoys them most?

- How intelligent are they? What does that cause them to do?

- Who knows their secrets?

- How do they feel about the bad things they do?

- What kind of dark settings would work well for this villain?

- Is this villain going to affect more than just my hero/heroine in the story?

- What is their favorite object/possession?

You don't have to answer all of these questions. They are meant to get you thinking about your villain, so that you can develop them more easily.

Villain Brainstorm #1

_____

_____

_____

_____

_____

_____

_____

Villain Brainstorm #2

_____

_____

_____

_____

_____

_____

_____

_____

Villain Brainstorm #3

_____

_____

_____

_____

_____

_____

_____

_____

## Villains And The Spiritual Truth Connection

Your Villain has the perfect opportunity to reveal a layer of spiritual (or inner) truth in your story. They might show the opposite of the truth in their behavior. For example, the revenge villain would be opposite of forgiveness. The reluctant villain will show the opposite of the concept that the truth will set you free. If I am doing a book with a spiritual theme, it is often helpful to pick a villain that shows the flip side of that spiritual truth.

When your villain embodies some lie the character believes, it allows the character to see the truth in their story by seeing the opposite behavior in the villain. It makes the character — and the reader — ask: Who do I want to be? Do I want to be like the villain who doesn't embrace the truth or do I want to be like the hero/heroine who is set free by the truth?

Showing the flip side of the spiritual truth through your villain will deepen your plot and your reader's understanding of the spiritual or inner thread of the novel.

# Idea Sparking

## Summary

In this chapter you have learned the different types of villains. You've taken some time to develop a few villains of your own to use in your novel. You've identified the spiritual or inner thread you want to showcase through the opposite example of the villain. Now, you will have an opportunity to select one, but before you do take time to read the next chapter because it deals with your villain.

# Ticking Stopwatch

As a little girl, waiting for Christmas was excruciating. The whole twelve days before crawled past with wish lists and Santa letters. Each day closer to Christmas, I got more and more excited. I dreamt of what would be under the Christmas tree and the treats we would eat. I dreamt of games and giggles, family time and movies. All of it part of the season that I loved, not to mention, NO SCHOOL! Until the night before when I could hardly even sleep. The anticipation kept me awake into the wee hours of the night tossing and turning.

Then came Christmas morning. The moment the sunlight hit me, I bolted out of bed and down the stairs ready to discover what was under the tree. All of the days leading up to this one, the tension had built to reach this high moment.

Writing is much the same way. Our character plods further and further into the story as tension builds toward one big event or climax. With Christmas, I knew when it was coming. Part of the tension for me was counting down the days until it finally arrived. For our characters, time can also play a huge role in the conflict in our novels.

# Countdown

One way a writer can use time to increase the conflict in their novel is by giving a countdown type of schedule. This occurs when it is a certain amount of time until your character must accomplish something, must save someone, or must catch someone. This information can be brought through a variety of characters.

You may have an informational character in your novel who spouts facts about the killer's pattern, including time references, that add tension to the novel. For example, a killer is killing every four days. Another time element to increase tension might be the amount of time someone is missing and the likelihood of finding them alive after 24 hours.

If your hero/heroine has a certain amount of time until something bad happens, that could also be considered a countdown element. For example, if he didn't make a house payment in the next ten days, they'd lose the house.

There may be a countdown in your story for how much time before you must save someone or catch someone. If they didn't catch the kidnapper in the next 24 hours and find out where he left the girl, she would be half-way across the ocean, the victim of a human trafficking ring. Another possibility, if they didn't find Ben in the next two hours he would freeze to death.

**Read the following story clip:**

*The field wouldn't plow itself, that's for sure. The sun scorched Tabitha's face as she pressed on behind Bessy. Overturned earth swirled in dust tornados and dissipated at the grass line like her late husband's dream for the farm.*

*Not two days had past since she laid her beloved in the ground, but life wouldn't wait for her to grieve. If the planting didn't get done this week, she wouldn't eat during winter, neither would the little one she cradled in her tummy.*

Here you get a sense for the importance of time. The story clip also establishes the stakes involved in the timetable. Please note, I did not use the phrase "time is running out" or anything like it. That is cliché and overused to the point that as I reader I get vastly annoyed with it, and I imagine I'm not alone. You can establish the countdown time conflict method without ever using that cliché phrase.

The countdown time conflict strategy in the story clip above can be formulated in this simple equation:

**Task + Deadline + Stakes = Countdown Time Conflict Method**

# Task

The first part of the equation involves the task the character needs to accomplish. In the suspense novel, it is usually involving a life-or-death situation, or catching a criminal. In other genres, it can be a task that threatens their livelihood, job, future, or heartbreak. Remember that the task must be directly tied into what the character values. Survival is a primal value that everyone has, but if the task is something they don't care about, neither will the reader.

**Read the following story clip:**

*Science was as interesting as counting ceiling dots. Tony slouched in his chair and tried to keep his head from dropping to his desk top. This class would never end. If he didn't get out of here soon, he'd be drooling. Not exactly impressive. He shifted in his seat. Five. More. Minutes.*

Here the equation is obvious. We have a task: staying awake. We have the stakes: drooling to embarrassment. We have the time: five more minutes. Still this whole thing falls a bit flat and shallow. We don't really care if he drools, and he sounds like a bit of loser. Let's try this again, but tweak it to have stronger stakes and maybe a bit stronger task conflict.

**Read the following clip:**

*Science was as interesting as counting ceiling dots, but impressing Mandy was worth every minute. If only he could get her attention. Maybe after class. He could carry her books to her locker, or something. Tony slouched in his chair and tried to keep his head from dropping to his desk. This class would never end. He had to beat Mr. Popular to the door, or his chances with Mandy were zero times a billion. Now to stay awake. Drooling and snoring didn't scream impressive. Come on Tony. Five. Little. Minutes...*

In this scene we care a lot more about Tony. Why? Because we empathize with him, we have increased the stakes and deepened the task. Let's take a look at our formula.

**Task:** Staying awake to beat Mr. Popular to Mandy's side **(Way more empathetic task.)**

**Deadline:** Five minutes till the bell rings **(Same as before.)**

**Stakes:** Mandy's Attention and His Embarrassment **(Very Powerful for a teenager.)**

Can you see how much of a difference it makes when we intensify the task and stakes to build more conflict in this scene? It is quite a simple strategy, but it really packs some punch. Let's look a bit more closely at the other components.

## Deadline

Giving your character a deadline for achieving a certain task will create more conflict in your novel. Do they need to come up with ransom money by twelve o'clock to save their loved one? Deadlines are specific and propel the character forward very similarly to the countdown.

You can also set up smaller deadlines in a story that lead up to a big one. That would escalate the tension in a progressive way. So, the bank opens at 8 a.m. and the heroine must be there. By nine o'clock she has to make the drop at a secured location. At ten o'clock the kidnapper will call with directions to find her son. At eleven o'clock a bomb that is strapped to her son will go off if they can't disarm it. Do you see the progression of deadlines?

This deadline progression works because the value challenges at each level or the stakes increase in impact. The big overarching deadline is to save her son before the kidnapper kills him. Along the way, we have the smaller ones: making it to the bank on time for the money, making the nine o'clock drop, be at the house to take a call from the kidnapper with directions, disarm the bomb or her son will die. The last one is a threat to the life of her son. This moment will grab her by the throat because she already did everything she could do to follow the kidnapper's directions. Even with all of her effort, her son could still die, and there is nothing she could do about it except trust the bomb expert.

Using a deadline can be a powerful way to make the conflict build in your novel. This strategy works with any genre, not just romantic suspense. Does your historical novel heroine need to get married in the next three days or lose her inheritance? Does your contemporary romance heroine need to find a date for a large company event or have to deal with the boss's unwelcome advances? Does you speculative fiction hero need to find the serum to reverse brainstem degeneration in five days or his whole tribe will die?

As you can see, deadlines work well in all genres to create conflict. Use the formula above to see if your novel could use the countdown time conflict strategy to up the conflict at key moments and keep your readers on the edge of their seats.

## Using Time Deadlines as a Distraction

Don't forget that you can utilize time deadlines to distract your character from seeing what is really going on. Like a bomb going off in another part of the city while a robbery is in progress somewhere else. It deflects the hero's/heroine's attention to the time deadline and keeps them from realizing the real problem. In this way, time can also add tension. How long will it take them to figure out what is really going on? And will it be too late to save the day?

## Ticking Stopwatch Stakes

One important technique for heightening time conflict is to give the time limit stakes. If your character has to get married in three days, be sure to include the stakes: or she will lose the family farm. If the killer is killing every two days, give the suspected victim a face (they've already gone missing). If she needed to convince the banker to loan her $400,000 then be sure to mention that they would kill her sister if she failed to acquire the money.

Without the stakes that make meeting the deadline or countdown so important, your time tension will lack punch. Be sure that the stakes you choose to increase tension have the maximum potential. Make the stakes affect something the character values.

**Read the following story clip:**

*Fire licked at the walls of Jeremy's bedroom. Had. To. Get. Out. Jeremy used his shirt sleeve to open his bedroom door and crouched below the smoke. Wailing came from down the hallway. He crawled across the hot floor stabbing his knees on shards of glass that must have come from the family photos on the wall. He ignored the pain and pressed on. A fit of coughing stopped his progress. Too. Far. He covered his mouth and nose with his shirt. Not much time before it was too late to escape.*

This story had a time deadline: before the fire got too hot and it was too late to escape. The story had a task: To escape the fire. When it came to the stakes, things fell flat. You might say, well he is fighting for his life. We know that, you don't need to say more. However, we missed an awesome opportunity to increase the stakes two-fold. Jeremy is the older brother, and his sister is wailing from her crib down the hall. He is trying to get to her before it is too late for either one of them to survive. We have just doubled the stakes. It can be a much more powerful scene with that in it.

## Practical Application

Now it is your turn. Rewrite the fire clip to include the doubled stakes. Add in more sensory details to intensify the deadline conflict. Build the panic by making his task more difficult (saving both his sister and himself).

_____

_____

_____

_____

_____

_____

_____

_____

_____

_____

Do you see the difference between the two scenes? There is a lot more conflict when you intensify the stakes, up the task difficulty, and use sensory punch to create a sense of urgency to the deadline. You can use this simple technique in flat scenes that seem to lack punch.

## Let's Review

The conflict countdown deadline strategy involves three steps:

**Task:** Make sure the task is meaningful. If not, up the level of difficulty to increase conflict.

**Deadline:** Give a specific deadline to when the task must be completed and strengthen it by giving sensory details and vivid imagery.

**Stakes:** Show what will happen if the character doesn't meet their goal or complete the task. Give a background of dread in the character to build the stakes.

## Apply

Brainstorm a list of countdown or deadline experiences you could use for your novel or a future novel. Be sure to add stakes to those for time tension impact.

_____

_____

_____

_____

_____

For each of the following, write the stakes that could make the countdown create more conflict.

**Corey needed to be home by five o'clock.**

_____

_____

**The photo shop closed in twelve minutes.**

_____

_____

**The car disappeared around the corner five minutes ago.**

_____

_____

The countdown time conflict strategy is as simple as utilizing the following equation, adding in as much conflict as possible in each component:

**Task + Deadline + Stakes = Countdown Time Conflict Strategy**

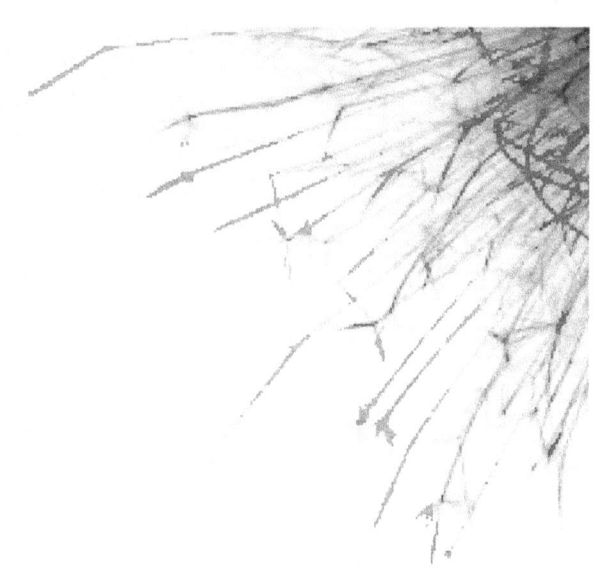

# Skyscraper Stakes

Growing up at my house as a young girl, my sister and I used to fight over the mixing beaters whenever my mom made cake. Picture two girls leaning against the counter, on either side of my mom, ready to pounce the minute she was finished. Yellow cake and angel food cake were okay. We would come out and wait for our chance at the finger-licking batter feast. And then there was chocolate. Chocolate required an all-out war for bowl, spoon, and mixing beaters. When my mom made chocolate cake, we came running, vying for the best possible position to move in. It should have mattered that my mom was on to us and always managed to give out equal amounts, but somehow we just had to push our way in to get the best of the treat.

When my mom made cake, my sister and I really cared about tasting the batter. It was something we valued at that age. What kid doesn't love sugar? But our favorite or most valued flavor was chocolate. So when the opportunity came for chocolate, we tried even harder to get the best of the batter.

Think of your character as a cake lover with values. In the case of your character, the cake is actually their quest or what they want to accomplish. It is what propels them forward into action to achieve their goals. As we covered earlier, a goal is what the character wants in the story or scene that they are in.

The flavor preferences of the cake are like the values of the character. My sister and I valued chocolate more than any other flavor. Your character has things in their life that they value more than others, such as loyalty, friendship, honesty, family, etc. Some things they will fight for more than others. These values drive their motivations for the action they will take to reach their goal. Motivation is simply the propelling force that compels a character to act. In other words, are you using the strongest values to produce the highest stakes?

The cake analogy is so easy to follow, so why is it so hard to use motivation and stakes in our novels? Sometimes we just don't know what is important to our characters, other times we don't know what our character really wants deep down inside. Either way, you can have your cake and eat it too. Your character can chase their dreams and face difficulties along the way, but with the proper motivation to create skyscraper stakes the conflict in your book will be thick as frosting.

## Overview of Skyscraper Stakes

In this chapter you will learn to identify and apply the key components of the skyscraper stakes equation. You will also learn how to build the stakes or maximize the stakes to the ultimate level to create more conflict on the page. The skyscraper stakes equation components include:

**Character Core Values:** These are the things your character values the most in their life.

**Character Motivation:** The reason a character chooses to behave the way they do is their motivation. Motivation is usually created by their values or their goals.

**Stakes:** Why something matters to a character is called the stakes.

# Character Core Values

We all have things that are important to us: our families, friends, job, loyalty, faith, intelligence, honesty, generosity. But there are certain things that are more important to us than others. In the cake analogy my sister and I valued chocolate more than the other flavors. Some people might like yellow or angel food cake better. It is individual to each person what they value most in life.

How do you get at what your character values most? Dig into their past with a character interview to figure out how they became who they are today and how that shaped their worldview. Someone who grows up impoverished is more likely to value money if they often went hungry. Someone who grows up in a broken home is more likely to doubt long-term commitment.

Ask your character, what do you believe is important in life? Why do you believe that? These questions will show you a character's core values. If they had to prioritize things in life, what would they put first, second, and third? (A more in-depth character interview can be found in Susan May Warren's *Inside Out*).

**For Example:**

*Curt had always dreamed of being a pilot, but when his father dies he is forced to skip college and support the family, including his ill mother. His younger sister left on her eighteenth birthday and never looked back. She enrolled in college and became a lawyer. Curt stayed at home and worked the same factory job for five years until his mother's debilitating disease finally claimed her life. He went to college, but stayed at the family home and tended his mother's favorite rose garden. When love found him in a small café down the block, he married a teacher who taught in a local elementary school.*

From this clip we can see that Curt has some strong core values. **Here are just a few:**

- Family means everything. You do everything for family.

- Loyalty

- Honoring the memories of the past

Each of these core values is important to Curt, but family at the top of the list. He has given up so much to put his family first, it is obvious that family is extremely important to him. Then you can see how loyal he is to his mother because he cares for her up until the day she dies even though he has dreams of his own. In the tending of his mother's rose garden, he preserves her memory and honors her. There are other core values we could find in this history such as responsibility or determination. The history of the character will build their core values.

## Practical Application

Now it is your turn to identify the core values of a character. Their history will tell you more about them. **Use the following character history to come up with five core values of this character.**

*Lucille Dunlap had grown up in the ghetto. The daughter of a single drug addict she spent many nights on the streets with her friends. Hunger drove her to learn to lift a wallet of a businessman in a matter of seconds. A life of macaroni and cheese and peanut butter didn't dim her courage.*

*When she turned sixteen, she drove her mother to the nearest treatment facility and dropped her off. She came home to an empty house and spent many nights awake listening to the shouts and blaring music from next door. Most nights she slipped off to sleep somewhere around four in the morning when her eyes were too tired to focus on the broken lock hanging on her apartment door. The rest of the nights, when it got to be too much, sshe'd invite a few friends to stay over. That's when she could finally sleep. Her dad's child support paid the rent, but Lucille picked up some side jobs in the neighborhood to buy food. Life was a cycle of survival and one day you died. That's what her mom used to tell her when she was a small girl. Now, Lucille believed her.*

From this clip, identify five of Lucille's core values.

_____

_____

_____

_____

_____

Finding a character's core values is the first level of scaffolding that creates skyscraper stakes. As you created the core values above, you developed the framework for the other two scaffolding levels of Skyscraper Stakes. Once you create character motivation and stakes, you will complete the three components of Skyscraper Stakes.

## Creating Character Motivation

A character is motivated by things that matter most to them, in other words, core values. They are also motivated by the goal at the end of the journey or noble quest they are on. Ask yourself, what does the character want to achieve by the end of the story? Why do they want to achieve this?

If you aren't sure of the answer to these questions, go back to the character's history. What in their past makes them who they are today?

**Read the following example:**

*Livy grew up in the richest neighborhood in town. Everything money could buy was at her fingertips, but there was no love in her home. Her parents fought incessantly and ignored her existence.*

*One day, she met a friend from the other side of town. He taught her what loyalty and friendship really meant. When she visited his house, she observed they all were happy and loved each other. She began to see that things didn't bring happiness. Still, she saw the homeless on the streets near her friend's house and children hungry waiting at the soup kitchen down the block.*

*When she graduated from high school, she determine to become a social worker and help those less fortunate. Her parents never understood her fascination with "that side of town." Livy moved out and now lives in the neighborhood where she serves the people who are struggling to get by.*

In this character history, we see Livy's core values in her decisions. She values people, happy families and serving others. Those things motivate her to take action and become a social worker and move to the side of town where she helps others. Livy wouldn't be motivated by money at all. If we try to create stakes that involve money, it will fall flat with this character because this is not what she values, it doesn't motivate her.

For this reason, it is extremely important to identify a character's core values so you can determine what motivates them. If the motivation you create for your character is not believable because it does not match who they are, the stakes will be weak in your novel.

# Practical Application

**Read the following character history:**

*Sam grew up in a blue collar family. His parents barely paid the bills each month. Whenever he needed something for school, they made do with hand-me-downs and thrift store goods. He held his shoes together with duct tape and wore a fall coat during the cold of winter.*

*His father worked as many hours as possible to put food on the table, so he rarely saw him during the week. His older brother picked on him a lot of the time, but otherwise they were a loving family. His parents did fight sometimes and when they did it was always about money.*

*Sam studied hard and got out of the neighborhood where he had lived and into a more affluent area. He worked, put himself through college, and got his medical degree. He bought a house in a rich neighborhood and flaunted his wealth with expensive cars and parties.*

What are some of Sam's core values?

_____

_____

_____

What will motivate Sam to take action?

_____

_____

_____

What will fail to provide a strong motivation for Sam?

_____

_____

_____

_____

Now that you understand the core values of a character and how they are motivated, let's take a look at how this will help us create skyscraper stakes.

## Developing Skyscraper Stakes

Stakes are the part of a story that answers the question, why is it important? The discovery of your character's core values and motivation has led us to this point of building the stakes higher and ratcheting up the tension. If the stakes are not high enough, our readers will get bored with our plot because if our character doesn't care about what might happen, neither will our readers.

**Read the following examples of stakes:**

## Example One:

**Core Value:**  Helping people is important.

**Motivation:** People are struggling and homeless.

**Stakes: (Why it matters?)** People will go hungry and die in the streets if no one helps.

## Example Two:

**Core Value:** Money equals success.

**Motivation:** Sam wants to be rich.

**Stakes: (Why it matters?)** Without money you will struggle your whole life to get by.

## Practical Application

### Character One

**Core Value:** Honesty.

**Motivation:** Honesty builds strong relationships.

**What are the Stakes?**

_____

_____

_____

### Character Two

**Core Value:** Spending quality time with those you love is important.

**Motivation:** Her mother is dying of cancer.

**What are the stakes?**

_____

_____

_____

## Skyscraper Stakes Equation

Let's take a moment to look at our cake analogy. The motivation for the rush to my mom's side as she was mixing the cake is impacted by the kind of cake that she was making. If she was making chocolate cake, we were more motivated to rush for the bowl because it was a special treat. Chocolate cake raised the stakes. If my mom operated on a first come, first serve basis that would build the stakes even higher.

Building the stakes is simply the equation:

**values + motivation + why it matters**

We can add the extra step of maximization (adding an increased level to why it matters) like I did above when I mentioned my mom operated on a first come, first serve basis. Here is how our cake equation works:

**Core Values:** My sister and I loved to eat cake batter.

**Motivation:** Licking the bowl and beaters met our need for cake batter.

**Stakes:** Getting there first meant you might get first pick of the beaters.

**Maximization:** Mom only gives the beaters to the first child who asks.

It seems so simple when we're talking about cake, but you can apply that same process to other parts of your book. Let's look at the character history of Livy again.

*Livy grew up in the richest neighborhood in town. Everything money could buy was at her fingertips, but there was no love in her home. Her parents fought incessantly and ignored her existence.*

*One day, she met a friend from the other side of town. He taught her what loyalty and friendship really meant. When she visited his house, they all were happy and loved each other. She began to see that things didn't bring happiness. Still, she saw the homeless on the streets near her friend's house and hungry children waiting at the soup kitchen down the street.*

*When she graduated from high school, she was determined to become a social worker and help those less fortunate. Her parents never understood her fascination with "that side of town." Livy moved out and lived in the neighborhood where she served the people who struggled to get by.*

## Applied Equation

- Her Core Values are generosity, people, and helping those in need.

  +

- Her Motivation is to help people because they are struggling.

  +

- The Stakes are that people are homeless and hungry.

  +

- The Maximization could be that there are not enough beds in homeless shelters for people to sleep in during the cold winter months.

  +

- Another Maximization could be that she has made friends with a homeless man who has nowhere to sleep. The winter months are coming and if they don't have enough social workers to open up a new shelter in that area of town, her friend could freeze to death.

As you can see, the stakes can continue to be raised over and over to maximize the plot potential. Livy cares that people aren't getting their basic needs met. Helping serve those in need is at the heart of her core values.

## Stakes of Loss

In some stories, the stakes have to do with the loss of a core value. This is often true in suspense, as well as other genres. The risk of losing love, a dream, or a family member can be powerful stakes in a story. The stakes of loss are usually higher than other types of stakes.

**Read this story clip:**

*Kara pulled her jacket hood tighter around her face and leaned into the wind. Her brother would pick a day like today to climb the side of a mountain. Snow crunched under her boots as she trudged up the steep incline. She had to find him.*

Is there anything wrong with that clip? No, but the more important question is, is there any conflict in that clip? You see, so many times we plant our characters in the scene, but forget the stakes. It seems active. She is climbing the side of a mountain to look for her brother in a snowstorm, but there is no intensity. **Let's switch it up a bit:**

*If she didn't find her brother, he might die on the side of the mountain. Kara pulled her jacket hood tighter around her face and leaned into the wind. Her brother would pick a day like today to climb the side of the mountain. Snow crunched under her boots as she trudged up the steep incline. She had to find him.*

The changes in the segment above add additional stakes by saying her brother could die in the snowstorm. Now we have life-and-death stakes that we know motivate Kara. But we can take it even a step further. Add some additional tension points to make reaching her goal of finding her brother even more difficult.

*If she didn't make the summit before the blizzard hit, her brother might die on this snow-covered slab of rock. Kara pulled her jacket hood tighter around her face and leaned into the wind. Snow crunched under her boots. He couldn't die today, not on the side of the mountain. Not when it was her all her fault.*

In this short clip you see that Kara is afraid to lose her brother. We maximize these stakes by the fact that it has a time limit and that today it would be her fault. We went from light stakes, to life-and-death stakes, to life and death stakes when time is critical and self blame is possible. Building the stakes of loss is powerful here. Kara has the potential to lose her brother if she is not able to beat the storm, and she has the potential to lose her ability to cope with her guilt if he dies.

## Practical Application

### Read the following story clip.

*The storm blew across the horizon in hues of blue and gray. Caroline needed to get the horses into the barn and get back to the house. She stopped the wagon in front of the barn and climbed down. Wind whipped her bonnet strings into her face. She hated storms.*

What are a few stakes of loss you could add to this to escalate the conflict?

_____

_____

_____

_____

_____

# Idea Sparking

Rewrite the clip to add in stakes of loss that escalate the conflict in the scene.

_____

_____

_____

_____

_____

_____

_____

_____

_____

**Summary**

It sometimes seems overwhelming to build the kind of skyscraper stakes that will keep your readers invested in the character's story. As an author if you break it down in smaller pieces by identifying the character's core values from their history, tapping into their motivations, creating stakes that matter and maximizing your stakes, it will be much easier to build the heighten and the stakes in your novel.

For the moments when you need the highest intensity of skyscraper stakes, try using the stakes of loss to draw your reader in and keep them reading late into the wee hours of the night.

# Switching Tracks

Life is like meatloaf, full of the unexpected. One minute you are planning a trip to the Bahamas with your husband, the next minute you are trading the travel brochures for *Baby Magazine*. You never know what kind of curveball life will throw you. What about your characters? Does life ever throw them a curveball?

As writers we plot our words to splash on the page, following plot points that travel in a straight line to the finish, but we forget our characters are human. I've done the same thing. Every once in a while I catch myself giving a character a charmed life. BORING!

As a reader, I want to find characters that struggle just like I do. As writers, we need to create those kinds of characters. Characters who have life events that cause them to switch tracks and go in a different direction.

## Diagnosing the Problem

Do you ever feel you are so close to your story that you have lost all perspective on its plot viability? I do. Sometimes I have to step back and look at it from a distance or get the help of a friend with strong plot skills. From this experience, I've developed a list of diagnostic tips that hint it is time for one of your characters to switch tracks. If you answer yes to any of the following questions, you may want to step back and switch tracks to make your character conflict more real:

- Does your plot flow in a straight line that makes it predictable?

- Do your critique buddies know what is going to happen before they read it?

- Are you struggling with a sagging middle? (When the middle of your novel loses the reader's interest, it is called a sagging middle.)

- Are you having trouble with character likability?

- Are your readers struggling to relate to your hero and heroine?

- Do your scenes end on a cheery note?

- Are you having difficulty finding the conflict in your plot?

- Are you having difficulty finding conflict to put in each scene?

- Is your word count too low, and you've run out of material?

- Have you forgotten to have your character make some tough decisions?

- Have the people in your character's life failed to impact your character's journey?

All of these questions can help you recognize the need to switch tracks in your character's plot journey to create more conflict. If you do not have any of those problems, you can still use the switching tracks technique to increase the conflict in your novel.

# Switching Tracks Strategy

Just like us, characters make decisions that shift the course of the story. They switch tracks and alter their direction. These changes can make for amazing twists and unexpected turns in our novels, if we learn to utilize them to their fullest potential.

There are many life events and emotions that make characters switch tracks. Think of your own life. Have you ever had a job opportunity in another state? Did your children decide to go to college five hundred miles away and you want to be closer to them? Have you done something you're not proud of to hide a secret? If so, your life has changed tracks. It has gone in an unexpected direction.

We can create unexpected events in our plot that affect our character in a way that they behave differently than they normally would. It will add conflict and keep our readers guessing.

As authors, switching tracks can be an effective strategy for widening the plot and building its intensity. Characters switch tracks for a variety of reasons: embarrassment, secrets, promises, and several other reasons. Let's look at a few of the most powerful ones for adding unpredictability to your plot.

## Embarrassment

Everyone in the world has experienced embarrassment at one time or another. Our characters should be no different. Embarrassment sometimes drives us to do unexpected things that readers can't predict when woven into the plot.

**Read the following clip:**

*If she survived this without making a fool of herself, it would be a miracle. Lucia climbed the stairs of the mansion on 243 Sycamore Lane. The heat of July blended with the scent of lilacs that swirled around her like bees circling honey ready to devour it. Lucia wiped sweaty palms on her pants and took a deep breath. She clutched her purse to her chest like a teddy bear. Her shaky hands reached out to touch the doorbell. It was find her courage now or go stag to prom. She rang the doorbell and waited.*

*Her stomach churned in a roll of revulsion. The door opened. Her eyes met the gorgeous baby blues she'd dreamed about each night for the past year. Handsome didn't do him justice. Lucia opened her mouth to say hi, but the word gurgled as she threw up all over his shoes.*

*What had she done?*

*Lucia turned and ran down the path. She wasn't going to prom. Not ever. And school? Not until she had to.*

In this story clip, Lucia goes to this boy's house to ask him to prom. She's nervous and can't even say hello before throwing up on the guy's shoes. That is a bit unexpected. Then she determines she is never going to prom or school again, if she can help it. That is how she changes tracks. Originally, her plan was to go to prom with a handsome boy she had a crush on. Now she doesn't even want to go to school.

Embarrassment is a strong motivator for our characters to switch tracks. For example, what if a man always wanted to date one of his colleagues? One day she invites him to go out dancing. He should say, yes, right? No. He declines. Why? He is embarrassed for her to find out that he doesn't know how to dance. This is a switching tracks moment, a moment when the character's actions don't mesh with the outcome because they are dealing with embarrassment.

# Practical Application

**Read the following clip.**

*"I know you are in there, Ryan." Mary pounded on the bathroom door again. "School starts in one hour."*

*"I don't care. Tell them I'm sick."*

*"Ryan Martin Caruthers, You open this door right now."*

###

From the story clip, give three possible reasons for embarrassment to switch Ryan's track.

---

---

---

---

Embarrassment can always raise the conflict in a scene because it pulls on reader's heart strings. They automatically empathize with the character. Embarrassment can help your character switch tracks to go in a different direction.

## Secrets

Everyone has secrets that they don't want anyone else to know. How about how much you weigh? Or the dumbest thing you've ever done? These are secrets you don't want anyone to know about, but sometimes secrets can be even more devastating to a character. Some secrets are so powerful that they keep us from doing what everyone would have expected us to do.

Characters switch tracks or direction in the story often because of secrets. The best way to use secrets is to make them larger than life. In other words, make the secrets threaten their way of life in a manner that cannot be put back together.

**Read the following clip.**

*If they found out the truth, she'd be charged with a murder she didn't commit. Elise grabbed the gun off the floor and tucked it in the back of her waistband, pulling her shirt down to conceal it. Her heart pounded. She swiped a hand across her sweaty brow. Time to disappear.*

Someone would have to have a powerful reason to steal a murder weapon from a crime scene. But Elise has secrets that can't be revealed or she will be charged with murder. Here are a few possibilities:

- Elise is working undercover and doesn't want to be questioned by the police. Since the original murder weapon was stolen from her apartment she would look really guilty and likely be made by the mob, wasting ten years of happiness.

- Elise bought the gun in her own name. Not only that, but she has a son whose prints might be on the gun.

- Elise shot the man in self defense, but she is the beneficiary of his large insurance policy. She believes that they will blame her for the murder.

In normal circumstances, Elise would go to the police, but because of her secrets she has kept vital information to herself. It creates a point of tension in the story because now the police are going to be looking for her.

## Practical Application

In the story above, Elise switched tracks and ran instead of going to the police. When she avoided being discovered it created unexpected tension. Every time you switch tracks the story's future is impacted.

**Read the following clip:**

*He'd never killed anyone before. Frank rubbed a hand over his forehead. The picture glared up at him from their dining room table of twenty years. All they had built their life upon and now this.*

From the story above, write three possible secrets that could make Frank decide to kill someone.

_____

_____

_____

_____

Frank has never killed before, so this is an unexpected twist that came from switching tracks.

An event from the outside or fringe plot came in to make him change directions. For example, his wife could have been kidnapped and he was told to make a hit or his wife would be killed. This would create a whole new dilemma in a character. They are likely to head in an unexpected direction.

## Promises

Another powerful motivation for a character to switch tracks is the promises they make to others. Have you ever promised something that was hard to deliver? I have. But our conscience tells us to follow through.

Our characters should be the same way. By giving them that human quality of wanting to keep their promises, we empathize with them. Keeping those promises may prompt your characters to do incredible things and go to incredible lengths. Their efforts to face difficulty to keep that promise is what escalates the tension.

**Read the following clip:**

*She vowed never to come back here again, but here Wendy sat parked in front of the largest estate on Periwinkle Drive in the middle of a downpour. All because she couldn't say no.*

*If she hadn't promised JD, she'd be half way to Memphis by now to start her new job.*

*Rain pelted the roof of her beat up Volvo like golf balls on a tin roof. Water streaked the windshield, blocking her view of the front of the house. Its sprawling three-story structure lay in the murky shadows of the trees lit by a solitary streetlight.*

*This place stuck its claws into anyone who stepped foot in the marble entryway, and never let go. It wasn't the first time she'd been summoned, but it would be the last. Today she'd set the record straight and be done with it. The old man might be dying, but she didn't want to be nailed in the coffin with him.*

*Her inheritance could go to a distant relative for all she cared. She wouldn't carry the baggage of the family's bankrupt soul.*

*Wendy pulled her raincoat hood over her head and pushed open the driver side door. The screech of metal on metal punctuated the slap* of the rain that pummeled the concrete. She slammed the door shut and sprinted for the house. The rain drenched her jeans and soaked into her shoes.

Wendy shoved the wrought iron gate open, catching her jacket on its latch. She gripped her jacket and yanked it closer to herself. The rip of fabric set her free, but a piece was left stuck in the gate. Couldn't worry about that now.

The house lay ahead in darkness, but for a small glow from the second story bedroom.

Wendy bolted up the sprawling white porch steps and stopped in front of the door. She might be out of the rain, but a storm wasn't always made of clouds and rain, but of flesh and blood.

She paused with her hand gripping the knocker. This time would be different. This time she would leave the next morning. This time not even JD could change her mind. She let the knocker fall against the door. Wendy shivered.

A light came on in the foyer. The door creaked open and JD stared down at her. The tangle of wild curls and dimples stole everyone's heart. If he hadn't been her brother, they might have stolen hers too. As it was, saying no to JD claimed every ounce of her resolve.

"'Bout time you got here, sis."

Wendy brushed past him and into the two-story foyer. Spinning on her heels, she reached up and gave him a hug. "Don't get used to it. I'm leaving tomorrow."

"Even if the old man writes you out of his will?"

"I'm done with his games."

"What if I told you someone was dying?" The light in his eyes turned somber.

*"What are you saying?"*

*"Daddy, are you going to tell her you have cancer?" A wobbly voice came from the top of the stairs.*

*Wendy spun around. A child no more than four tucked her head around the corner. Her large brown eyes and wild brunette curls struck Wendy right in the heart. She wasn't going anywhere. Not today. Not anytime soon.*

Wendy starts this scene planning to leave as soon as she can, but by the end of the scene she has switched tracks. She is staying right where she is for an indefinite amount of time. This is an example of how promises can change the total direction of your character's journey. If her brother didn't have cancer and a child she had never met, Wendy would be back in Nashville by the end of the next day. Now, she is thrown into a situation where she might be staying in town with her brother for an undetermined amount of time.

## Practical Application

In the story above, we see how Wendy switches tracks when something unexpected comes her way that has to do with a promise she made to her brother JD to come home. By the end of the scene, the plot is heading in a totally different direction.

**Read the following story clip:**

*Sneaking past the guard looked like the only option, but he didn't have to like it. Gabe flattened his back against the side of the ship's wall. The metal grid of the battle station pressed into the palms of his hands. The faint odor of dumpster rot rose from the steam farther down the compression chamber where the empress had disappeared.*

*When he swore to protect her with his life, he had no idea she'd test that oath every day. Now, he was chasing her through an enemy ship with nothing but his bare hands to protect her, that was if he could even find her.*

Give three unexpected things that could happen as a result of Gabe's promise to the emperor to protect the empress.

_____

_____

_____

_____

## Avoiding Trouble

In most of our lives we try to avoid trouble. Think of your character as the driver of a car in rush hour. If there is a driver in front of him who stops so suddenly that he can't react in time, he will often swerve to the side. Plot is the same way. Your characters drive the plot just as if driving a car. As we throw a conflict in front of them, they will swerve to miss it. By avoiding trouble, they change the whole direction of the plot and switch tracks.

**Read the following story clip:**

*One hour before the exchange. Denny shoved the cash into a duffle bag, all fifty thousand dollars. He was on his own this time. No police. No backup. He zipped the duffle bag shut and anchored the strap over his shoulder. Time to get his baby girl back.*

Here we see that Denny is going to pay a ransom without calling the police. This is not the norm for an individual facing this situation. They usually call police to help them. What are some possible reasons that Denny would choose to avoid the police?

- There is an outstanding warrant for his arrest, and he doesn't want to get caught.

- The villain has threatened to hurt his daughter if he involves the police.

- He doesn't plan to let the villain live. He plans to kill him and not get caught.

These are all possibilities when we throw conflict at our characters and try to get them to swerve or switch tracks to avoid the trouble. There are lots of different ways we can use this scenario, not just in suspense.

**Read the following story clip:**

*There was no way he could go in there and come out alive. Sam shoved his baseball cap lower over his eyes. Mr. Obenhimer's house stood looming above the trees. The smell of lilacs clogged the morning air. Girl scent, yuck.*

*A window on the first floor shuddered with movement. Sam backed away. His heart pounded in his chest. He crouched lower behind the bush. No baseball was worth that much.*

Give three examples of what Sam might do to avoid trouble in this scene?

_____

_____

_____

_____

In this story clip, Sam is afraid to go to the big house and get his baseball. That may encourage him to take on a paper route to pay for a new one. Or, he might pay someone else to get it for him. There are lots of possibilities for causing our characters to avoid danger by switching tracks.

## Personal Sacrifice

Have you ever had to make a difficult choice because it was good for someone else? How about the last time you went out of your way so your child could be part of a special program, or event? When these difficult choices are big enough, they often make our characters switch tracks.

**Read the following clip:**

*This town killed a wildflower's spirit. Ruth Kramer ought to know that. Her chance to get out of here had come and gone. She rested her palm on her tummy. But now...*

*Ruth lifted her hand to shield the sun that blistered the Texas dirt. Not much here worth staying for. Wasn't like Jeb would have anything to do with her now. Besides if she left town today, she might have a scrap of self-respect left. Didn't matter that she hadn't said "yes." It was all the same out here.*

*No baby of hers was going to grow up in this town. Not while she had breath left in her.*

In the story clip, we see that Ruth might have stayed in the town where she was living but now that she is expecting a baby, she wouldn't. She didn't want to risk her child facing the same things she had to face. Being pregnant changed the way she looked at life. To bring about good for her baby, she would leave this town behind. Her baby's best interest is a powerful enough motive to go, even though it seems she loved a man named Jeb.

## Practical Application

*The blue cloth matched her eyes perfectly. Maybe even Clay would notice. Mary smoothed the fabric spread across the patchwork quilt. The soft folds, smooth under her work worn fingers.*

*"Auntie Mary..." Clare ran into the room, her cheeks rosy from running. When she got to the edge of the bed, she stopped. Her eyes widened.*

Give three personal sacrifices that Mary could make to switch plot tracks based on this part of the story. Think about more than just the moment, but the bigger plot implications it might have.

_____

_____

_____

_____

_____

_____

Select one of these and rewrite the scene to help Mary change her plot track.

_____

_____

_____

_____

_____

_____

_____

_____

_____

_____

## Summary

Conflict builds in a novel when the unexpected comes in to change the direction our character is going. By switching tracks due to motivations that aren't always anticipated by the reader, an author can create unexpected twists and turns that keep the reader flipping pages till late into the night. We can use our character's secret need to avoid embarrassment or danger, to keep their promises, and to bring about something good to change the direction of their plot journey. Switching tracks creates surprise for the reader and makes the story more enjoyable.

# Cliff Hangers and the Happily Ever After

I'm a big fan of the happily-ever-after movement. You know, where the handsome prince comes in and saves the princess and carries her back to his castle. Sigh.

Wait a minute, the prince forgot to mention dirty dishes, laundry, ironing, (if anyone still does that... thank goodness for wrinkle-free) trash day and toilet cleaning. Don't even get me started.

The guy who invented happily ever after is sitting in his castle somewhere laughing his head off. Amazingly enough, I can't stand anything less at the end of book...Thanks a lot mister!

So where exactly does the happily ever after go? It should come at the end of the novel. But where do we stick it sometimes? We put it at the end of a scene or chapter.

Are you guilty of putting happily ever after where cliffhangers should be?

We've all been there from time to time, but let's look at cliffhangers and how to use them to motivate readers to keep reading.

Cliffhangers are the last line or two at the end of a scene or chapter that leave a reader hanging. It's what makes them stay awake at night to read because they can't put it down. Strategically, your best cliffhangers should come at the end of a chapter. It also pays to put them at the end of a scene.

## Identifying the Problem

No scene or chapter should end in a happy moment unless it is the end of the book. If you solve your character's problems, why would anyone need to keep reading? Having your character or plot problem resolved in a scene is fine, but you must introduce a new problem at the end. If not, the reader will think it is a great place to take a break and put the book down. Sometimes they don't pick it back up.

The end of a scene needs something to propel the reader to the next scene, but even more so the end of the chapter must get the reader interested in the following chapter.

**Here are some examples of final paragraphs for a scene or chapter.**

*Today tested her courage. She met the challenge. Now it was time to lie down and rest. Callie lay back and put her head on the pillow. The soft glow of the hallway light warmed her skin. She slipped into a deep sleep.*

*The moon glared down on the sidewalk in front of Laura. She shouldn't be out here this late at night. The echo of a bullet sliding into the chamber brought on the shivers. The time for wishing she'd waited for Ben wouldn't change the inevitable. She was here alone, in the dark. And her killer had her in his sights.*

*The district attorney had already made his case against the defense. It didn't look good. The jury swallowed every word like a piece of prime steak. Sandra's client didn't have a chance in the world. Her defense started tomorrow. He'd fry if she didn't find something to go on.*

*The date was perfect. She'd found prince charming. He even seemed to like her too. Christy hugged the pillow to her chest. Darren was her prince, and he was here to stay.*

Which of the final paragraph clips held more conflict and draw to read more? Paragraphs two and three make us wonder what the character is going to do. These paragraphs leave the character in a problem that is hard to resolve easily. Paragraphs one and four imply that the the character will be okay. It is all good. Nothing to fear. What we are looking for here is the tension we find in paragraphs two and three.

I know you might be thinking your genre doesn't lend itself to cliffhangers like a suspense novel, but no matter the genre you can create one. Let's try this with paragraphs one and four.

## Paragraph One:

*Today tested her courage. She met the challenge. Now it was time to lie down and rest. Callie lay back and put her head on the pillow. The soft glow of the hallway light warmed her skin. She slipped into a deep sleep.*

**Let's rewrite it:**

*Today tested her courage. She met the challenge. Now it was time to lie down and rest. Callie lay back and put her head on the pillow. The soft glow of the hallway light warmed her skin, but it wasn't enough to chase back the shadows. She'd survived today, but what about tomorrow?*

Do you see how very quickly this is changed into a drive forward to the next scene? Now we want to know more about tomorrow and would she ever be able to chase back the shadows. Now we want to know more about tomorrow and if she would ever be able to chase back the shadows.

## Paragraph Four:

*The date was perfect. She'd found prince charming. He even seemed to like her too. Christy hugged the pillow to her chest. Darren was her prince, and he was here to stay.*

**Let's rewrite it:**

*The date was perfect. She'd found prince charming. Christy hugged the pillow to her chest. Darren was her prince charming. He even seemed to like her too. What would happen when he found out her secret? Prince Charming would turn into a frog like always. He couldn't find out, or she'd lose him forever.*

We used the initial story segment to pull out the why not of the romance. Or we hint at what is coming. Now we all want to know what her secret is and if Prince Charming will dump her. Authors are often tempted to give away secrets too early. In this clip, I could have divulged what the secret was, but then I would have lost some of the tension. It is better to hold the secret until the scene where it is needed. Sometimes, authors even manage to hold a secret for several chapters while the readers are dying to know what it is. That is what we want our cliffhangers to do.

By now you're probably saying, I have "happily-ever-after"-itis. I can't write a cliffhanger to save my life. I know how you feel. When I first started writing, I left happy moments at the end of every scene. But that took all the conflict out, so I started studying cliffhangers and how to make them. I will share what I learned with you and before you know it, it will be simple for you too.

## Creating a Cliffhanger in Three Easy Steps:

First, identify the problem the POV character has going forward from this scene.

**For example:** *Sally sprinted toward the bank. The clock struck twelve. Five minutes before the deadline. She entered the bank lobby and approached the teller. Just in time.* (Sally's Problem: She is running of out time.)

Secondly, stop writing the scene before you resolve this problem, or you must introduce a new one. So, you should stop the scene at the line: Five minutes before the deadline.

And finally, add a line to give it punch. **Why does it matter?**

**For example:** *Sally sprinted toward the bank. The clock struck twelve. Five minutes before the deadline. If she didn't make it in time, her husband would die.*

Cliffhangers are merely made up of the ending problem of the POV character and a punch line that tells us why it matters. Not all of your scenes will be as dramatic as this one, but you should try to find the strongest cliffhangers to end your chapters.

**Step One:** Identify the problem the POV character has going forward from this scene.

**For example:** *Ben looked at the balance in his checking account again. It wasn't enough to buy a ring, but if he kept saving he could buy it in three months and propose.*

**The Main Problem Ben Has Going Forward:** He doesn't have money to buy the ring.

**Step Two:** Stop writing the scene before you have resolved the problem or you will have to introduce a new one.

**For example:** *Ben looked at the balance in his checking account again. It wasn't enough to buy a ring.* (Notice here I dropped the line about him being able to save up for three months and then he could buy it. When I give a solution to Ben's problem, I removed the conflict. Even if that is true, I don't have to state it right here.)

**Step Three:** Add a line to give it punch. **Why does it matter?**

**For example:** *Ben looked at the balance in his checking account again. It wasn't enough to buy a ring. In three months Liz was moving to Montana to start a new job, unless he could show her their commitment was serious. He needed that ring.* (Here I have added a line or two to give the problem punch. It matters because she is moving, and he needs to show her he is willing to commit or he will lose her.)

The story examples have much more tension when we follow the cliffhanger method to develop conflict at the end of each scene and chapter. It is a simple method to follow, and anyone can do it.

# Practical Application

Now it's your turn. Using the three-step method, develop the following paragraphs to have a cliffhanger ending.

*Destiny fought the joy that buoyed her spirits toward the clouds. Just looking up into his face was all it took. Her heart thawed and opened to the possibility of the man of her dreams standing right in front of her.*

**Rewrite the paragraph above using the following steps:**

**Step One:** Identify the problem the point of view character has going forward in the story.

**Step Two:** Stop writing before you resolve the problem, or you will need to introduce a new conflict.

**Step Three:** Add a line to give it punch. **Why does it matter?**

_____

_____

_____

_____

_____

_____

_____

_____

_____

# Idea Sparking

*He's finally behind bars. Heather pushed the hair out of her face and yanked open her car door. The beat-up interior of her car attested to it's age, but the smell inside came from only one man. Now, he had been put away for good.*

**Rewrite the paragraph above using the following steps.**

**Step One:** Identify the problem the point of view character has going forward in the story.

**Step Two:** Stop writing before you resolve the problem, or you will need to introduce a new conflict.

**Step Three:** Add a line to give it punch. **Why does it matter?**

_____

_____

_____

_____

_____

_____

_____

**Summary**

Cliffhangers are a key part of building conflict in our novels in a way that readers want to keep reading. Using the three-step method, you can go through each of your scenes and replace happy endings with the cliffhanger that will bring more tension.

# PART THREE
Combining Strategies

# Diagnosing the Problem

In my years growing up, fairness mattered. My sister and I fought to even the fair factor all the time. Kids today haven't changed. They want everything to be fair, but that is just not possible. If Kara falls and breaks her leg, she goes to the doctor. In the waiting room, she might meet up with a boy named Seth who has the flu. If Kara gets a cast does that mean Seth should get one too? No. That's ridiculous. The doctor knows how to treat a patient to cure the problem, not to be fair.

Our manuscripts are the same way. If we see something wrong it doesn't always require the same solution, so it is important to learn to diagnose the problem correctly. By now, you may be panicking and breaking out in hives. I can relate. Sometimes I feel red pen impaired, too. But take a deep breath. We will go step by step through common conflict problems in a novel and have checklists to identify the problem. From those checklists, you will have a sense for what needs a cure. If you know what is wrong, it is so much easier to find the right strategy to solve the problem. Let's begin.

## Big Scale Conflict Concerns

To start our diagnosis, we will look at the overall story conflict. This encompasses the whole novel, not just individual scenes. As a point of reference, if the structure off, your story is off these strate-gies will not fix that problem. These strategies are more focused on the conflict components of your overall novel. If you are concerned about story structure problems, you can find helpful information in Susan May Warren's *From the Inside...Out: discover, create and publish the novel inside of you.*

When we look at the whole novel to determine if you have brain-stormed enough conflict for your characters there are some basic questions you can ask yourself. These questions will lead you to a brainstorming strategy that can help you with this problem. Just as a doctor would ask you questions to assess your current condition and identify the problem, we will follow that strategy to assess your manuscript's current condition and identify possible problems.

By no means will you use each and every strategy in every book you write. You may choose to use several of them, but just because one is missing doesn't mean you have to add it in. If you tried to add every strategy to every book it might be overwhelming, but adding a few to build the conflict in your novel will strengthen your story's punch. You can determine if there is a problem with certain parts of your story's conflict by asking the following questions:

**Big Scale Conflict Questionnaire**

- Is your story predictable? (Can your critique readers guess what is coming next?)

- Does your character have a boring life?

- Do you have a plot plateau in the middle where the difficul-ties do not escalate?

- Is your character able to face the challenges of life with everyone on their side?

- Does your character live above the scope of real life difficul-ties?

- Does your character have difficulty making decisions or do they make seemingly stupid decisions?

- Does your hero/heroine's fear seem unrealistic?

- Is your character self-involved?

- Are you backed into a plot corner?

- Do all of your character's difficulties involve plenty of time to resolve?

- Is your character able to avoid situations that would require them to choose between values?

- Are your character's actions predictable throughout the whole book?

If you answered yes to any of the above questions, you may have a Big Scale Conflict issue in your novel. If you answered yes to several of the questions, you definitely need to take another look at the conflict in your novel. Don't fret. In the next chapter, we will address each of these questions with a possible strategy guide to let you know which conflict strategies might correct the problem. If you passed with flying colors, ask a critique buddy or two to answer the questions about your novel. They may respond differently.

The questionnaire above will help you determine if you have overall plot conflict issues in your novel. What about those individual scenes? We have covered several strategies in this book that are also helpful with small scale conflict that we find in individual scenes. By small scale conflict, I don't mean that the conflict is light. It is just looking at a smaller snapshot of your novel, just on the scene level. Let's take a look at some red flags that might appear in individual scenes to show lack of conflict impact.

# Idea Sparking

### Small Scale Scene Conflict Questionnaire

- Is my character goal in this scene clearly separate from my author goal?

- Does my character face obstacles to the goal they have in this scene?

- Does my character have obvious stakes, or something to lose if they don't reach the goal?

- Does the scene have internal conflict?

- Does the scene have external conflict?

- Does the scene end on the edge of a cliff where the reader needs to keep reading?

If you answered no to any of the questions above, it is likely you have a conflict problem in your scene. Individual scene conflict issues are a bit easier to remedy than the overall novel conflict, but it is still important to learn to recognize these problems or they could make your whole novel lack impact one scene at a time. In the final chapter we will dig into the questions of small scale conflict difficulty and help you identify the strategies that will address some of the sluggish conflict impact.

## Let's Review

There are two basic conflict diagnostic tools that will help identify the lack of conflict impact in your novel. The big scale conflict questionnaire will diagnose issues relating to the story as a whole. While the small scale conflict questionnaire will diagnose issues related to individual scenes. Both of these areas are important to deliver a conflict-filled story that the reader can't put down. Now that we've diagnosed the problem, let's get to work finding the solutions.

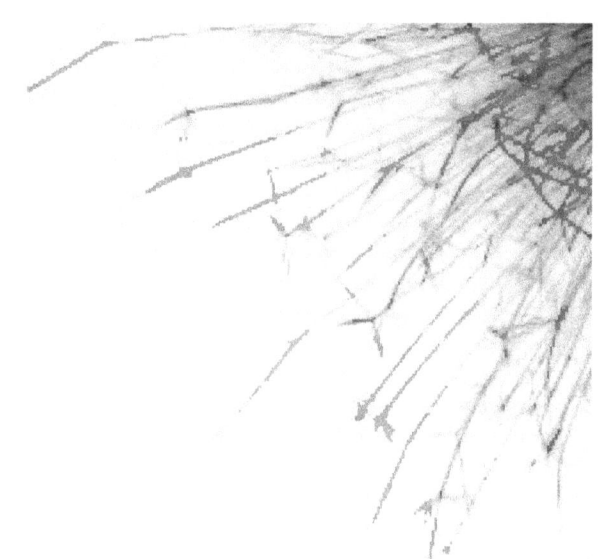

# Big-Scale Conflict Solutions

We learned the formula for brainstorming conflict in our novels in the first section of this book and how the three components of our fire equation can intensify your novel's conflict and eventually make its popularity spread like wildfire.

**Flint + Tinder + Metal Friction Sparks = Fire**

**OR**

**Idea + Character Goals + Stakes + Obstacles = Conflict**

We've covered basic brainstorming strategies, and how to identify character goals and develop the balance of internal and external conflict in our novels to create sparks. We've learned and practiced several individual brainstorming strategies to find meaningful conflict. We've even learned to diagnose potential conflict problems in your novel. Now, it's time to apply what you've learned to your own work.

There is no need for panic. You can rest assured that we will take it a step at a time and you will be applying these skills like a pro. Using the Big-Scale Conflict Questionnaire, we can evaluate your manuscript by each individual question and give you some possible strategies that strategically address the weak conflict areas. Let's get started.

# Solutions for "Yes" Answers on the Big-Scale Conflict Questionnaire

## Is your story predictable?

This question basically addresses whether your reader knows what is going to happen before it does, or if you fail to surprise your reader during the story. Sometimes we only think of being unpredictable, but there is also a delight in surprises. Readers often will talk about a novel that took an unexpected twist. So let's fight predictability and add in a few surprises for our readers. The following strategies work well if your story is too predictable:

**Boomerang-** Taking what is expected and doing the opposite.

**Secret Sabotage-** Using character secrets to bring about unexpected actions from a character.

**Villain Scouting-** It makes the story more unpredictable when you have an outside person fighting against our character's goals. It will create conflict in unexpected moments.

**Switching Tracks-** Letting life impact your character and force them to switch directions for a better good.

These four strategies are particularly useful in creating unpredictable plot conflict and a few surprises along the way. You may choose to use one of these or all of them, but predictability is something that needs to be addressed, not ignored. If you can't remember the strategy just go back and review it when you need to use it.

## Does your character have a boring life?

Boring characters will put a reader to sleep faster than counting sheep. You need to be aware of your character being too vanilla, or too much like your other characters. Do your characters dither or make seemingly stupid decisions? Then your character has a boring life in the reader's eyes, because they don't feel real. Here are some strategies that work best when your character has a boring life:

**Conflict Escalation Strategy or Mountains vs. Plateaus-** This strategy will help build conflict escalation in your novel. Whenever you escalate the conflict for your character, it takes some of the yawn out of the world.

**Pedestal Principles-** When a character, or someone they relate to everyday have unrealistic expectations of that character it creates additional conflict and empathy in readers.

**Secret Sabotage-** Little secrets create believability in our characters. To see them struggle with difficult decisions, and to have made past mistakes, makes them endearing to the reader.

**Villain Scouting/Graveside Manner-** I put these together here because they work in tandem with each other. When you have a dull character, pitting someone else against them can showcase their strong qualities that readers like.

**Switching Tracks-** This adds unexpected direction in the character's journey and makes them feel more real to our readers.

**Cliffhangers and Lullabies-** A character may seem boring if everything always works out for them at the end of every scene or chapter. Applying the Cliffhanger building method will help to lessen the sense of "everything is fine, so why do I care?" in your readers.

When a character leads a boring life, these strategies can breathe new adventure into the story and create more conflict to keep the reader interested in what is happening on the page. Bringing the unexpected and unforeseen challenges to your character and maximizing the presentation style of your character's story will add depth and conflict to your novel.

## Do you have a plot plateau in the middle where the difficulties do not escalate?

Anytime you have a sagging middle in your plot, there is usually a problem with escalating the conflict from one challenge to the next. In order for the plot to keep building to a climax, you must escalate the conflict. All of the strategies in this book will have some impact on middle sag, but here are a few strategies you might want to try:

**Conflict Escalation Strategy or Mountains vs. Plateau-** will enable you to increase the conflict with each disaster that happens to your character and escalate the sagging middle into a mountain peak.

**Mirror Reality-** Creating a parallel of the hero's/heroine's greatest fear as it happens to a secondary character magnifies the reality of the undesirable outcome. This strategy is packed with conflict potential both internally and externally, feeding into the escalation effect.

**Ticking Stopwatch-** Consider using countdowns to create conflict as time runs out. This will create the escalation of conflict as the time before the deadline draws near.

**Skyscraper Stakes-** This method escalates the stakes (what a character has to lose in the story) as the plot grows, creating an escalating conflict that often eliminates middle sag.

**Cliffhangers and Lullabies-** When your chapters and scenes end on a happy note, you steal the tension that can move a novel forward. When a chapter ends with a cliffhanger, the conflict propels readers to keep turning pages.

A sagging middle turns away readers like a luke-warm chocolate malt. Using these strategies to escalate the plot in a mountain formation, and presenting each new conflict in the most meaningful way possible will create more conflict on the page and get rid of the spare tire that is occupying Act Two of your novel.

## Is your character able to face the challenges of life with everyone on their side?

Real life is full of adversity and adversaries a lot of the time. If your character lives a charmed life and everyone is on their side, the reader won't relate to them. It's important to create conflict, both in life situations and between characters, to build the story conflict. If your character has everyone on their side, here are some strategies you might want to try:

**Pedestal Principles**- In real life sometimes people around us have unrealistic expectations of us. When we try to please them, this causes conflict. Use this strategy to build that type of conflict for your character.

**Secrete Sabotage**- Characters, like real life people, have secrets they don't want revealed about themselves or their past. By creating a secret broker, or someone who threatens to expose the character's secrets, you build conflict. It also makes us as readers want to rally behind them, because we have all been there.

**Villain Scouting**- If your character is living a charmed life, it may be time to find a villain in the story that opposes them and raises the conflict. In every genre, there is potential for a villain that can complicate the character's journey.

**Graveside Manner**- If we feel like the character has everyone on their side, it may be time to point out that their opposition is powerful. Using the Graveside Manner technique will raise the conflict by showing the reader how dangerous your villain really is to the character.

You may be the most popular person in the world, but you will still have enemies. Not everyone is going to love you, some may hate you just because you are successful. Not everyone will adore our characters either, no matter how lovable. Readers enjoy cheering for the underdog. Give them the chance by creating adversaries to their goals that are both dangerous and smart.

## Does your character live above the scope of real life difficulties?

Characters are empathetic when we like and relate to them. Having real-life difficulties makes readers want to cheer the characters on and hope for the best. Consider these strategies for building conflicts that make your characters seem real:

**Pedestal Principles-** Creating unrealistic goals set by our character, or those around them, builds conflict and empathy. We all understand what it is like to feel like you will never be able to meet the expectations of others.

**Switching Tracks-** Life events happens unexpectedly. When something unanticipated comes our way, we change to accommodate the new situation. Characters seem real when they also have to switch tracks, creating more conflict in the plot.

**Secret Sabotage-** We have all done things in our lives that we are not proud of and sometimes we would do anything to hide that from the rest of the world. Our character has made mistakes in their past or has flaws they'd like to keep hidden, too. When we show this side to our characters it makes them take on skin.

Characters living a charmed life don't create a very strong story unless something them shakes upand propels them toward a change. By creating real-life dilemmas for our characters, using the strategies above, we allow them to join the real world and build a fanbase among our readers.

# Does your character have difficulty making decisions, or does s/he make seemingly stupid decisions?

A character who can't make decisions, or one who makes poor decisions, will drive a reader bonkers. Readers will either think the character is stupid or that s/he's not living in reality. Most readers like a character who knows what they want and goes after it. If your character seems indecisive or makes seemingly stupid decisions, here are a few strategies you might try:

**Secret Sabotage-** Sometimes your plot requires a character to do something that makes no sense. Utilizing the Secret Sabotage Strategy will empower you to give your characters reasonable motivations for their actions.

**Skyscraper Stakes-** If we haven't adequately built in the character stakes leading to their actions we often feel the character is making poor decisions. Using the Skyscraper Stakes method will help you build the motivation for actions and often utilize the conflict of two core values to create a motivation for the desired action.

We see enough indecisive leaders and poor decision making in real life. Readers want heros/heroines who are decisive. By utilizing the strategies above, we build motivation for our character's actions and get them to dive into the real world with their own ideas about life.

# Does your hero's/heroine's fear seem unrealistic?

Characters need to have a worthy adversary in the story in order to build the sense of real fear and danger. If we want to establish this fear in a realistic way, we must show how dangerous their adversary is and how the circumstances warrant their fear. Here are a few strategies you might try if your hero's/heroine's fear seems unrealistic:

**Mirror Reality-** Allowing the worst case scenario to happen to someone close to your character makes that possibility seem much more likely and showcases the horrible outcome. This will build the character's fear legitimately because they will naturally worry that if this situation could happen to someone they know, it could happen to them.

**Villain Scouting-** If you don't have a threatening enough adversary to your character's goals it is helpful to search your cast of characters for a possible villain who fits your genre and builds conflict for your character. Having a villain embody the challenges your character faces, makes the conflict more real for the reader.

**Graveside Manner-** Building the villain's competence at being wicked or successful at opposing the character's goals makes the fear more believable. Developing a dangerous persona can build the conflict around the fear to escalate the tension.

**Ticking Stopwatch-** Increasing the chances of the character reaching their goal in time will add more realistic fear. Even if a person had to raise ransom money, the timeline would increase the difficulty level immensely.

**Skyscraper Stakes-** By building the stakes (what the character has to lose if they don't reach their goal), we increase the fear component. If they have more to lose, it is natural for them to have a greater element of fear.

If there is no real danger of our character failing to reach their goals, then there is no real story, in our novel. Character change is at the heart of story, and without a strong enough catalyst to force our character to change, their motivation will seem unbelievable.. Utilizing the strategies above you will create realistic fear of our character's inability to reach their goals.

## Is your character self-involved?

A self-involved character is difficult to like. Let's face it, no one wants to be with someone who only talks about themselves and only thinks about their own agenda. Still, it is so easy for us to inadvertantly build that type of character. We have our characters spend so much time in self-absorbed thought and all of the conflict is about them. If your character is difficult to like, here are a few strategies to try:

**Switching Tracks-** Let life come along and shake your character out of their comfort zone and cause them to make sacrificial choices for those they love, putting another person's needs in front of their own.

Self-involved characters are often not empathetic to our readers. Utilizing the Switching Tracks strategy, we force our characters to get actively involved in other's lives. Instead of obsessing over their own thought world, they will choose to do things that are better for others. This creates a more likeable character whom readers can root for.

## Are you backed into a plot corner?

Perhaps you have plotted yourself right into a corner where there is no action your character could take that would seem believable without derailing your whole plot. Usually when this happens, it's time to reexamine the character motivations and possible fringe plotting options. If you are backed into a plot corner, try the following strategies:

**Boomerang-** You may be trying too hard to think of a clever way out of that plot corner, but the solution may just be as simple as doing the opposite of what is expected.

**Secret Sabotage-** If you can't think of a good reason for your character to do what you want them to do, create a secret and a person or situation who could reveal it. That often allows you to have characters do something that doesn't make sense, but will get you out of a plot corner.

**Skyscraper Stakes-** When there is no way your character would take the action you need them to take to get out of your plot corner, you can create logic out of the illogical by giving motivation for the actions. Have your character choose between two core values that, when pitted against each other, force a decision that furthers your plot.

**Switching Tracks-** If you've backed your character into a plot corner, bringing in fringe plot (external plot from other characters or life itself) can create a reasonable shift in plot direction that creates new conflict.

Utilizing the four strategies above will give you the potential to get out of the plot corner your character has backed into a believable way. These strategies can also create additional conflicts and unexpected twists in your novel.

## Do all of your character's difficulties involve adequate of time to resolve?

Time is a luxury that allows a character to work slowly at a problem to find a solution, but there isn't nearly the conflict potential in this plan. With the right amount of time, a lot of unfathomable things become an outside possibility. To avoid giving your character the luxury of a limitless deadline, try the following strategy:

**Ticking Stopwatch-** Give your character a deadline that makes it extremely difficult for them to reach their goal.

By utilizing this strategy, you will increase the potential for conflict exponentially and drive the plot forward with a sense of urgency that keeps a reader turning pages.

## Is your character able to avoid situations that would require them to choose between values?

Our core values do not always go cohesively side by side. Sometimes we must choose between them in order to continue on with life. It isn't always easy, but it is necessary. If you haven't created this dilemma for your character, you will miss out on an opportunity to create conflict and a connection with the reader. To force your character to choose between core values, try the following strategies:

**Secret Sabotage-** When you value keeping your secrets of your past from ruining your future, you many have to choose between the two. Does something about your character's past, if revealed, threaten their future? And do they value telling the truth? This would be an example of how Secret Sabotage could impact a character's decisions.

**Skyscraper Stakes-** To increase the stakes we often force a character to chose between two core values. This will escalate the conflict in the story.

Forcing a character to choose between two core values helps us as writers build motivation for our character's actions and create external as well as internal conflict. Utilizing these strategies will maximize our conflict potential throughout the novel.

## Does your character do anything unexpected in your story?

If you know exactly what is going to happen in a story, do you want to read it? Only if the way they get to the ending is unexpected, right? Personally, I want all of the books I read to have something unexpected in them. I want to be surprised. Have you given the readers a surprise? If you are looking to create a dash of the unexpected, here are a few strategies to try:

**Boomerang-** Just when the reader thinks they know exactly what is going to happen, you twist the story around and come right back at them. This creates a delightful surprise.

**Secret Sabotage-** When your hero/heroine is trying to hide something from someone, they often do things that don't make sense to other characters unless they know the hero's/heroine's secret. These unexpected actions can create surprise for the reader.

**Switching Tracks-** Bringing in bits of peripheral or outside plot to impact our character often creates an unexpected surprise.

Give your reader the gift of unwrapping your story. Don't let them know what exactly is going to happen. Keep them guessing and they will come back for more time and again. Build surprise into your novel for the readers who cherish that challenge.

## Let's Review

The Diagnostic Big-Scale Conflict Questionnaire may have uncovered some weaknesses in the conflict of your novel. Although the strategies in this book can be used for many of your conflict weaknesses, some are more suited to solving certain problems than others. Those strategies are listed above to guide you as you work on ramping up the Big-Scale conflict in your novel.

Remember, you can always refer back to this reference to help you in the future, so there is no need to worry about being able to utilize them from your memory. Take time to apply and practice these techniques over and over. You will find these strategies will become much easier with practice and will give you the skills you need to deepen the conflict in your novel.

# Small-Scale Conflict Solutions

As we learned in the previous chapter, there are multiple strategies that can be used to solve the conflict problems in your novel. Many of the strategies in this book can be overlapped and applied to address different concerns. The focus of our previous chapter involved looking at strategies that are helpful for solving big-scale conflict concerns. The discussion in this chapter will focus on small-scale conflict solutions for individual scenes.

Each scene requires conflict to build a strong propelling force that rushes your story towards the climax. If a scene doesn't move the story forward, it should be eliminated. If you have a scene that is necessary to the story, but the Diagnostic Small-Scale Conflict Questionnaire raised some concerns then it is time to take a look at some possible cures to your dilemma. We will follow each small-scale conflict question to determine some of the possible cures you can implement to solve the problem.

# Solutions for "No" Answers on the Small-Scale Conflict Questionnaire

## Does my character's goal in this scene stand clear of my author goal?

Remember early on in the book we discussed the difference between an author goal and character goals. An author goal is the goal you as an author have for this scene, what you want to accomplish. A character goal is what your character wants to accomplish in this scene. If your character goals are absent, add them into your scene so you can create obstacles or conflict to stand in the way of their goals. If necessary, review the first few chapters of this book to help you implement this method.

## Does my character face obstacles to the goal they have in this scene?

Once you have identified the character goal for the scene, it is time to evaluate if your obstacles match your character goals. If they don't, your scene will lack strong conflict. Remember, obstacles are the roadblocks that stand between your character and what they want to accomplish in that scene. These roadblocks should be aimed at the character goal, or it will be like setting up roadblocks to catch a criminal on a different highway other than their escape route. Refine the obstacles to match your character's goals and build conflict in the scene.

## Does my character have obvious stakes, or something to lose, if they don't reach the goal?

This question gets at the heart of "why should I care?" Why should the reader or character care if they don't meet their goals? Remember stakes are what your character has to lose if they don't reach the goals they set out to reach at the beginning of the scene. The stakes should be big enough to matter to both the character and the reader or they will fall flat. Refine and build the stakes to create stronger conflict in your scene. Show what they have to lose in a palpable way.

## Does the scene have internal conflict?

For a scene to be balanced, it must include both internal and external conflict. Remember, internal conflict is the turmoil that goes on inside the character. It shows us what they are thinking and their emotions. It gives us a deeper sense of the character's Point of View. Without internal conflict the hero/heroine will feel wooden and may not be as empathetic to the reader. The internal conflict is also the directional piece of the character's journey to change, so without it our story will lack substance.

## Does the scene have external conflict?

External conflict balances the internal conflict in the scene to create the perfect mix of action and emotions. Remember, external conflict is the turmoil that goes on in the world around the character and makes life difficult. External conflict causes the challenges the character must face in order to create a need to change or opportunity to change in the character's life. Without the external conflict, our character will lack believable change that comes only from facing challenges and learning to overcome them with new truth.

# Idea Sparking

## Does the scene end on the edge of a cliff where the reader needs to keep reading?

Happily ever after is the stuff that the end of books are made of, but at the end of each scene and chapter the reader should be worried about the character. Remember, cliffhangers are the last line or two of a scene or chapter that makes a reader what to know what is going to happen next. Ending a scene at a place that makes our readers concerned about our characters adds additional conflict to our novels and creates in the reader a hunger to keep turning the pages.

**Three-Step Method to Creating Cliffhangers:**

**Step One:** Identify the problem the point of view character has going forward in the story.

**Step Two:** Stop writing before you resolve the problem or you will need to introduce a new conflict.

**Step Three:** Add a line to give it punch. **Why does it matter?**

## Let's Review

In order for a scene to have the necessary conflict to escalate the plot in a mountain formation it must include the components mentioned above. Remember that there are other additional things that a scene should include in order to have the maximum impact, but in this book our focus has been on brainstorming conflict. At each step in creating a scene, be sure to ask yourself these questions about the conflict you have created and you will find your scenes contain more punch and greater purpose in the whole scheme of your novel.

# Conclusion

In this book you have discovered the power of brainstorming conflict for your novel. You've practiced applying strategies in small steps to intensify conflict. You've even learned how to diagnose problems with the diagnostic questionnaires and match solutions to the difficulty you are experiencing.

Is your mind a jumble with great ideas, but confused with where to go from here? Take a deep breath. All of the strategies we have learned here are available on your shelf next to your writing desk. Let's pull it all back together and put things into prospective so you can move forward with confidence in the new conflict-building strategies you've learned.

Brainstorming conflict in your novel can be the spark that lights a fire in your fiction. It will draw readers and loyal fans as they learn you pack punch in your plot. They will be excited to pick up your next novel because they have come to expect decisive characters with escalating conflict and high stakes. Remember our fire equation from the beginning of the book?

**Flint + Tinder + Metal Friction Sparks = Fire**

**OR**

**Ideas + Character Goals + Stakes + Obstacles = Fire.**

Each of these steps we studied in greater depth to prepare you for implementing the strategies we learned in Part Two of this book. Below is a brief review of the components of the equation.

## Brainstorming

Brainstorming is what gets all of the fire building started. It is the flint that you use to build a bank of ideas. There are a few steps to brainstorming that are important to remember:

- **Don't Censor Your Ideas.** Allow your mind to explore all ideas without judging them.

- **Blurt In A Continuous Stream.** Let the ideas roll without any thought in between.

- **Don't Stop Too Early.** You may have come up with a great idea, but don't stop there.

- **Brainstorm in Small Chunks.** Brainstorming should focus on small things in the story.

Using these brainstorming basics prepares you for the great ideas to come pouring out. The more free you are in your brainstorming, the more amazing the outcome of each session.

## Character Goals

The basic goals we have set up for our character or the things they are trying to achieve, provides fuel to build the fire once sparks start flying. Introducing idea sparks without the framework of character goals creates a plot that lacks conflict.

Conflict is the roadblock to your character's goals in the story. Some conflict affects one scene, other conflict affects multiple scenes. In individual scenes these roadblocks are called obstacles.

These obstacles, or conflicts, stand in the way of your character reaching their scene goals.

There are three key components to each scene that will set up the framework for conflict: **Goals, Obstacles, and Stakes.**

**The Three-Tier Framework for Building Meaningful Conflict:**

**Goals-** This is the POV Character's goal in the scene. (Not the author goal.)

**Obstacles-** Things that get in the way of the POV Character achieving their scene goal.

**Stakes-** What is at stake for them in this scene? What will happen if they don't achieve their goal?

When you are able to identify the character goals, it opens up the opportunity to maximize the impact of conflict in the story. It is this three-tier framework that allows us to build all brainstormed conflict into our novel in a meaningful way.

## Conflict Strategies

There are two kinds of conflict in a novel. Internal conflict is the turmoil or conflict from inside a character which often fuels the character's journey to change. External conflict comes from the surrounding plot challenges outside of the character that helps propel them toward change. Balancing external and internal conflict in our novel allows us to pack punch in the conflict we include.

In Part Two we looked at twelve strategies to brainstorm conflict in our novels. Each strategy provided a variety of conflict opportunities. The following strategies were included: Conflict Escalation Strategy/Mountains vs. Plateaus, Boomerang, Mirror Reality, Pedestal Principals, Secret Sabotage, Villain Scouting, Graveside Manner, Ticking Stopwatch, Skyscraper Stakes, Switching Tracks and Cliffhangers vs. Lullabies. Each time you need help brainstorming conflict, you can pull out these strategies and give them a try.

## Diagnostics and Solutions

In Part Three you learned how to diagnose potential problems in your novel that leave conflict weakness. Using the Big-Scale Conflict Diagnostic Questionnaire, you were able to identify problems in the story conflict as a whole. Utilizing the Small-Scale Conflict Diagnostic Questionnaire, you were able to identify conflict gaps in individual scenes in your novel. Each of these questionnaires provide a powerful assessment tool to analyze the conflict in your novel and its impact on the story.

Once you identified problems with the conflict questionnaires, we provided possible solutions for the difficulty you were facing in both your individual scenes and stories. These follow-up suggestions from the questionnaires can be used as a guide to fix sagging plot, unlikeable characters, blank page dilemma and a wide range of other plot conflict issues.

## Where Do I Go From Here?

You have taken the step to build a new type of brainstorming in your writing life. I encourage you to brainstorm something every day to get your mind involved in the story even before you put thoughts on the page. When you are plotting conflict for your novel, try the strategies you learned in this book. After finishing a scene, utilize the Small-Scale Conflict Questionnaire to make sure the conflict is maximized for the most powerful outcome. When you get stuck in plot corners or need help to brainstorming conflict, pull out a few strategies from this book. Follow-up with the Big-Scale Conflict Diagnostic Questionnaire to verify that you have avoided a conflict plateau.

As you begin utilizing the tools in this book, you will be amazed at how it revolutionizes your writing. You can build meaningful conflict in your novel. So, strap on your computer chair, roll up your sleeves, and get ready to start a fire with your characters.

# Glossary Words

**Anger Flashes-** when villains lose their temper and have the ability to rage.

**Author Goal-** what the author wants to accomplish in a scene.

**Big Scale Conflict-** refers to the conflict that is across the whole layout of the manuscript and involves multiple scenes.

**Boomerang-** A strategy that involves doing the opposite of what is expected in the story to build conflict.

**Carnal Knowledge-** Knowledge of weapons, or tools of wickedness, crime scene clean-up.

**Chameleon Capabilities-** The villain's ability to blend in and be like everyone else.

**Character's Core Values-** These are the values most important to your character. They address the very core of what a character believes.

**Character Goal-** What a character wants to accomplish in a scene or in the whole book.

**Character Motivation-** Why a character behaves the way they do. Things that motivate them to action.

**Charm-** The villain manipulates others to him/her because of the villain's suave abilities.

**Cliffhanger-** The final few sentences of a scene or chapter that leave the character in a place of conflict, making the reader want to find out what is next.

**Concept Villain-** Things that keep our characters apart like war or distance.

**Conflict-** Roadblocks or obstacles to your character's goals.

**Conflict Escalation Strategy-** A brainstorming strategy that transforms plot plateau into conflict that escalates in mountain formation.

**Countdown Time Conflict Strategy-** Utilize the following equation to build conflict in your novel:

**Task + Deadline + Stakes = Conflict**

**Dark and Twisted Villain-** A purely evil villain such as a sociopath or psychopath.

**External Conflict-** Conflict that comes from outside of the character usually is the result of things that happen or challenges they have to face.

**Fire Equation-** Utilize the following equation to build conflict in your novel: **Brainstorming + Character Goals + Conflict Idea Sparks = Fire**

**Flint-** Brainstorming is the flint that helps us to create fire in our novels. When applied to the other components of the fire equation it generates a powerful outcome.

**Fringe Plot Conflict-** This is conflict that comes from the outside of the story on its edges that are unexpected but believable.

**Goals-** What a character wants to accomplish in a novel or an individual scene.

**Good Intensions Villain-** A villain who means well but causes trouble for the hero/heroine by their actions.

**Graveside Manner-** A wicked way the villain acts to add tension to our story.

**Internal Conflict-** Conflict that comes from inside a character and often fuels their spiritual journey.

**Maximization-** A strategy that builds the stakes higher to get the most conflict punch in a scene.

**Mirror Reality-** A strategy that involves showing the hero's/heroine's worst fear coming true in the life of someone they know to build conflict.

**Obstacles-** The roadblocks to your character's goals in a scene.

**Physical Villains-** A type of villain that attacks the body like cancer, or a virus.

**Point of View-** The character's perspective we are in during a scene. The POV character is the one who is acting out the story and we can see what they are thinking and feel their emotions. (Should be one per scene.)

**Position of Power-** If the villain is in a position that gives them power over the way things happen; such as law enforcement, government officials, employers, etc.

**Proximity-** The villain is close to the victim. Maybe they are in the same circle of friends, or same work place. A way to give the villain easier access to the victim.

**Reluctant Villain-** A villain who does not want to do bad things, but is forced to because of something that is at stake for them.

**Repeat Offender-** If the villain has done this before. The hero/heroine doesn't need to know it, but the reader does. It will build tension in the reader.

**Revenge Villain-** This villain is full of hate and unforgiveness, and that is what fuels their behavior.

**Secret Sabotage-** A strategy that uses secrets to create conflict and unexpected actions in a character.

**Skyscraper Stakes-** A strategy that builds the stakes or what the character has to lose to create more intense conflict.

**Small-Scale Conflict-** This refers to the conflict you find in individual scenes of a book.

**Sparks-** In our fire equation, these are the conflict ideas that start a fire in our novel.

**Stakes-** What a character has to lose if they do not reach their goal.

**Switching Tracks-** A conflict-building strategy that utilizes peripheral or external plot to build twists and new conflict for our characters.

**Tension-** The combination of internal and external conflict in the story that makes the reader care about our characters.

**Ticking Stopwatch-** A strategy that involves using time or a deadline to increase the tension in the story.

**Tinder-** The things you find in your story to use as fuel for the spark once the fire is lit. Basic goals and stakes are the tinder in the fire equation.

**Villain's Dangerous Traits-** Characteristics that make a villain dangerous in a way that builds conflict for our character.

**Villain's Lair-** The place the villain goes to plot evil or save trophies of his/her crimes.